PETTY CUPID

SARAH BLUE

FOREWORD

Hello, welcome to Petty Cupid.

If you would like a full list of the contents in this book please
visit authorsarahblue.com/content-warnings

If you're not a fan of the term *Daddy* you can return the book and
we can both act like this never happened.

PLAYLIST

Love On The Brain - Rihanna
The Summoning - Sleep Token
Lover - Taylor Swift
DEATH - Melanie Martinez
Truly Madly Deeply - Savage Garden
Somewhere Only We Know - Keane
Lavender Haze - Taylor Swift
My Love Mine All Mine - Mitski

For Juliet

I really hope that your life turned around after shoplifting panties at DEB while we were at the King of Prussia Mall for bible camp and you got sent home and I never saw you again.

Xoxo

"All right, Cupids. The big day is in three days. Make as many matches as you can before the love year resets!" my ex-boyfriend says to the massive crowd, where we're all gathered in Cupidale for our weekly huddle.

Fucking the boss was absolutely a bad idea.

Not only is Eros a complete tool, but his new flavor of the month, Juliet, stands to his right. Only two weeks ago, it was me standing there.

It's not that I'm devastated over not being with him, I just hate this feeling of being so easily forgettable.

But I'm not the new cupid on the block. In fact, I'm up for the Seductress of the Year Award, and he loathes that. Eros is only happy when he's the center of attention.

He broke up with me the day the nominees were announced.

I thought maybe he'd be proud of me and support me just like I did when he won the Fuck Boy Award last year. Yes, there is absolutely an award for that. I know it's drab, yet also completely fitting for the beaming male cupid in front of me. He isn't handsome anymore, when I look at him all I feel is stupidity for ever letting him dig his perfectly pink manicured nails into me.

Well not really, Eros wasn't completely into the things I am, yet I stayed, and I feel like an idiot for it. You'd think that since he's the boss he would be dominant in bed. Definitely not, if anything he's more of a pillow prince, and that's absolutely not what I want long term. If anyone should be getting the royal treatment in bed, it's me.

But as soon as he saw that I wasn't the naïve little cupid that needed a big strong man telling me how to do my job, he dropped me. Broke up with me without even blinking, hardly gave me an explanation. The bastard even called it mutual uncoupling. For using that phrase alone, I truly want to make him pay.

Deep down, I know I'm better for it, I deserve someone better. Someone who likes me for me, who is supportive, and who can give me what I truly need in a relationship. Which includes someone who isn't afraid to take charge and put me first for a change. Eros only thinks about what he wants—I'm pretty sure he jerks off while looking in a mirror.

But did he really have to break up with me two weeks before the Valentine's Day Ball?

The event is the biggest day of the year for cupids. The ghosts have Halloween; the angels have Christmas, and I'm not sure what the reapers have, but they must have some morbid celebration one day a year.

But there's no way that their celebrations are anywhere near as good as the Love New Year. We celebrate with absolute debauchery, and now I have to go solo. Only the dud cupids go to the Valentine's Day Ball solo, or the ones that are really into group stuff. Sadly, I find I get overstimulated with more than one set of hands on me.

Cupids spend months planning their wardrobe and making plans for this event. I already have a dress, I'm up for an award, I have no other option but to go. I really want to put itching powder in his tighty-pinkies just for the simple fact that I'm now scrambling for a date to the event.

Only a real asshole breaks up with someone—specifically a cupid—right before Valentine's Day.

"What a fucking prick," Amore says next to me.

"You can say that again."

"What a fucking prick," she repeats and I smile.

"What am I going to do, Amore? I've asked nearly all the cupids I know, and they already have dates to the ball. I can't not go, I'm up for an award. But there's no way in hell I can go solo. Not when he'll be with Juliet. I'll look like the pathetic stupid cupid who got dumped while he raw dogs her in the corner of the venue."

Amore snickers and shakes her head. I'm not kidding that I've asked just about every cupid if they're free—that probably doesn't help my case for looking absolutely desperate. God, I want Eros to suffer. While winning the award will be a solid slap in the face, I need it to really hurt. He needs to realize I'm the one who's doing better after the relationship.

"Every cupid already has a date?"

"Every single one I know, yes." I sigh dramatically, watching as Eros wraps his arms around Juliet. The poor new cupid has no idea what she signed up for. I suppose I didn't either.

That's how the bastard gets you, with his perfectly quaffed pink hair, and sparkly pink skin. Not to mention he has a special plated quiver and bow because he's upper management. Which really is just nepotism in its highest form. He didn't truly earn his spot managing the cupids within the Milky Way; he was given the position by his father. And boy does the cocky son of a bitch use it to his advantage.

Fuck him and his special quiver and bow. Because I can tell you from experience, his real quiver (if you know what I mean) is nothing to write home about.

I'm seething as I stare at him. I hate feeling foolish, but most of all I *loathe* feeling used. I watch people fall in love all day, and I desperately want it for myself. But as I look around the room full of cupids who are in relationships or other entanglements, I can't help but feel a little hopeless. Like I don't belong. Eros breaking up with me just magnified that tenfold.

"What if you didn't bring a cupid?"

"What do you mean?" I ask, furrowing my brows at Amore.

"A different immortal in the veil," she says with a shrug.

Her hair is a darker shade of pink that's braided and wrapped around her head. She's taller than me too, and her pink skin is more of a raspberry shade to my bubblegum pink.

I swallow and blink at her. *Is that even legal?*

"I thought only cupids could come to the event," I reply.

"It's just a thought. And according to the bylaws, that is in fact, not true," Amore says. I swear she knows everything when it comes to being a cupid. She's a great friend to have, not only because she always takes my side but because she holds a mass wealth of knowledge.

I love her, and truly wish we were each other's type, but alas, we are soul mates of a different form. Love comes in many shapes and sizes, and I'm honored to love her in such a comforting, platonic way.

"I'll keep asking around," I reply to her, as Eros and Juliet walk up to us through the crowded white meeting space.

I swallow and remind myself that revenge takes time. Simply shoving an arrow up his butt in front of everyone would likely get me fired, or worse. No, I've got to be smart about how I handle this. The last thing I want is everyone thinking that I'm acting out because he shattered my heart into a million pieces. No, he didn't have that effect on me or my lady bits. Just my fragile little ego.

"Your numbers have been down this past week, Love. I hope I didn't have anything to do with that," Eros says with a toothy grin. Juliet laughs at his joke.

Asshole.

His jab doesn't sting as much when I remember that I'll no longer be having subpar sex with a narcissistic, misogynistic douchebag.

I give them both a polite smile back and tilt my head.

"No, I've just been very busy handling my own lust, if you know what I mean." The lie flows off my tongue easily, and Eros's face falls.

Good. Knocking him down a peg feels so fucking good. It's probably not cupid or lady-like, but the idea of hurting his ego as much as he hurt mine lights a fire under me.

"Certainly not so soon," he replies.

The smile on his face is one of a man who is a fraction away from losing his shit. I love it. Maybe I could make his head pop off.

"He had just been waiting for me to get back on the market. As soon as he found out I was single, he asked me out on a date. It's been wonderful."

Juliet clicks her tongue, her hand on her hips as her pink wings flare behind her. "That's great that you found someone new, seeing as Eros and I are together."

Part of me wants to pat her head and buy her a vibrator because there's no way she's getting off. Instead, I smile. I had to learn the hard way, and I suppose she has to as well.

"Exactly. He'll be at the ball. You can meet him then."

The lies just sweep off of me like they mean nothing but watching his face contort makes it worth it, even if I'm digging myself into a giant gaping hole I can't dig myself out of.

"He will?" Amore says questioningly.

"He will."

Eros bops my nose with his pointer finger.

"Good for you, kid."

A dark part of me wants to tilt my chin and bite his finger off. I'd even swallow it so that he couldn't magically attach it somehow. I know we're immortal, so I'm not sure what the rules of dismemberment are, but I'm willing to find out.

Eros and Juliet walk away and I look over at a wide-eyed Amore.

"So what's it going to be? Angel, ghost, or reaper?"

I grimace. "I guess let's start from the top of the list and work our way down?"

"What if you can't find anyone?" Amore says.

"Then I'll have to find a way to kill myself."

Amore belts out a laugh and shakes her head. "Listen, if you can't find anyone, you can come as a triad with me and Doe."

"Thanks, Amore, but I specifically said I was coming with a guy."

"Something you didn't do with Eros," she claps back and I laugh.

"Definitely not. Part of me feels sorry for Juliet. She doesn't know who she's dating. "

"Well, you have three days to find someone and keep up with your quota."

"I might give a couple of cupids a heart attack if I actually pull this off," I say.

"We can only hope."

"All right, well here goes nothing."

I teleport to Target, a common hang out of the angels, so I can shoot my shot.

The front aisles are covered in teddy bears, flowers, and skimpy lingerie.

It's beautiful.

Valentine's Day truly is the best, and I will not let the cupid version of a pile of trash ruin this holiday for me. Maybe while I'm here, I can shoot some lust or love arrows.

As I walk down the aisle, I see a man holding two bouquets and I can't help but think how precious it is that he's buying his lover so many flowers. Love is certainly not dead, at least not on Earth. From what I've heard from other cupids some of the other planets are truly struggling. I know I'm fortunate to work on this planet, and I take my job very seriously.

If there's anything I can take pride in, it's knowing that I'm a good cupid. My senses are sharp, and my aim is immaculate. I smile to myself, the tension from Eros' rude words leaving me as I watch the humans shop for their lovers.

His friend walks over, and they laugh together.

"I'll drop one off to Parvati in the morning and the other to Hannah in the evening," he says.

"You're a pig, you know that?" I shout out at him, knowing he won't hear me.

Humans are lucky that they don't hear all the horrible things we say about them, because sometimes they can truly be awful. The only thing that keeps me going is the true love matches. That's what makes being a cupid worth it. And the amount of fucking these people do, that also makes it totally worth it. I might be a bit of a voyeur, but such is life as a cupid.

I want to shoot Parvati and Hannah with love arrows to fall in love with each other and ditch this scum bag. There's truly nothing better than a love match between two scorned love interests. Maybe I'm a tad more petty in nature than I realized.

I make a mental note to circle back to that potential love match between the two unknowing girlfriends, but I'm angel hunting. I need a date more than I need to teach this cheating frat-bro a lesson.

I find two male angels and two female angels hanging out in the decor aisle. All of them look at me suspiciously and I give them a wide smile. While I'm perfectly pink all over, they are shimmering with gold.

Pretty.

The cupids would lose their fucking minds if I were able to snag one of these gold studs for the ball. Gold against pink would look absolutely stunning, and plus it's no secret that cupids are considered a lesser form of angel. I'd say we're no less important though. What's the world without a little love?

"Hi there," I say with a wave.

"Oh, just ignore her and maybe she'll go away," one of the female angels says.

Well, that's very un-angelic.

"Nice setup you have here. It smells like at least eighty different types of candles," I blurt out, not knowing what to say. How do I tell them I would like one of them to come with me to a party that always turns out to be an orgy in order to make my ex-boyfriend jealous?

Wait... do angels have sex?

"Do angels have sex?" I ask and they all gasp, scandalized. So… I guess that's a no. *Shit.*

"Heavens help me," the one male angel says, teleporting away.

"I forgot how blasphemous cupids were."

"Without love or lust the humans wouldn't fuck like bunnies and reproduce, and you wouldn't have a job either, pal," I reply, wanting to take a lust arrow out so they can realize how awesome sex is.

"What do you want, cupid?" the other male says boredly.

None of them would survive a second at the Valentine's Day Ball, a bunch of golden prudes if I ever saw one.

"Nothing, never mind." I sigh.

"Thank God we're not cupids," they jest behind my back as I walk away.

Angels are kind of dicks.

Feeling defeated, I walk down the gorgeous, capitalistic aisles of love at Target. I can't even enjoy all the red, pink, and cute. This is a tragedy, truly. Valentine's Day is the best time of the year, and here I am on an impossible mission surrounded by loveless people.

The pig who's cheating on two women is in the checkout lane and I just can't help myself as I pull out two lust arrows, hitting him and the friend he's with. Truly, they deserve one another. The two men kiss each other frantically, and I can't help but wonder if there was an underlying feeling of desire over the way they're going at it.

Maybe he'll leave those poor girls alone and they can find someone better for Valentine's Day.

This did not go the way I planned at all. Angels were really my best option to show up Eros and create a tsunami of jealousy among the cupids.

But honestly, the angels are such a buzzkill. I guess I would be too if I weren't getting laid and my only job was to be a holier-than-thou narc. They aren't a good match for the Valentine's Day ball so now I have to go down the list to the next immortal being.

Ghosts.

Could a ghost even touch me?

There's only one way to find out. I teleport directly to the closest graveyard. There are multiple dreary looking ghosts milling about and I consider which one to approach.

A handsome man, sitting cross-legged on a tombstone, catches my attention and I walk in his direction. He's lighting a ghostly cigarette as he looks up at me.

"Cupid," he greets me plainly.

"I didn't know ghosts smoked," I say stupidly.

"I'm already dead, cupid," he jokes, shaking his head, inhaling the cigarette. The smoke goes nowhere.

Great… Now, where do I go next in this conversation?

"You're a quite handsome ghost," I tell him.

He smirks. He's got a bad boy look to him, see-through ghost leather jacket and all. I'm sure he was a serious heart breaker when he was alive in this realm. I guess I should be morally opposed to a man who spat on the foundations of love in his previous life… but he is very pretty.

"You don't belong in a graveyard, cupid."

"Love, my name's Love. Also... I don't know, this is a very nice graveyard you have here," I flirt.

"Usually the visitors we get are a little more alive and a lot weepier," he states.

While I suppose my appearance is a huge adjustment to the poor humans who come here in mourning, I hope that he'll be able to help me. I've only been here in the veil for a little over a year, so I don't know much about the other beings who also live here and interact with the humans.

"What's your name?" I ask, trying to appear even more friendly in hopes of snagging myself a very hot, dead date.

The ghost looks me up, and down like he likes what he sees, definitely a good start.

"Rich," he replies.

"That's a nice name. Really screams you have money and that you'd treat a lady right," I reply, turning on the charm.

"Cut to the chase, cupid," he says boredly.

"Rich, you seem like a straight shooter, so I'm going to give it to you straight. My ex-boyfriend dumped me for a brand new, naïve cupid and we have the biggest celebration of the year in three days. It's Valentine's Day, you know? Anyway, he was being a particularly awful asshole to me, and I came up with a lie that I had a date when I really don't. All the other cupids already have dates for the ball and I obviously can't bring a human, so I thought asking a fellow immortal in the veil would be my best option. I'm up for an award, you know? That's the whole reason he broke up with me, because he can't stand the idea of a powerful woman. So, I want to bring another hot immortal to the party and show him what he's missing out on," I say it so rapidly that I'm nearly out of breath, and Rich the ghost grins at me.

"I wish I could help you out, Love. But unfortunately, I can't leave this spot, nor could I touch you." He clicks his tongue. "Which truly is a shame."

I groan dramatically. He would have been perfect and I totally would have let this ghostly hottie at least feel me up. "You really are a hot ghost, you know?"

He laughs and sighs. "This is truly unfortunate."

"Any other ideas?" I ask him.

"How do you feel about death, cupid?" he asks, somehow arching his ghostly brow as he throws his cigarette and it fades into nothing.

I swallow thickly and shrug my shoulders as Rich gives me directions to my last and only hope.

I need to track down a reaper and pray that they won't smite me or laugh right in my face when I ask them to be my date for Valentine's Day.

*H*anging out around a hospital seems like an incredibly fucked-up place to find a date. But Rich told me this would be my best bet, souls are collected here multiple times a day to be ferried to their final resting place.

Follow the departing souls, nab a reaper. How hard can it be?

A reaper can touch me, isn't a prude, and absolutely would make Eros shit his pants. Honestly, the cupid community as a whole might lose their ever-loving minds.

It's perfect.

Walking into the Valentine's Day Ball with a reaper on my arm is the perfect play. I don't know why they were on the bottom of my list. Maybe I felt a little put off by the whole death and doom thing, but truly, they would make the biggest statement—that I'm not to be fucked with.

One of them zooms by, down the halls, their black cloak trailing them. They're the embodiment of death and about as antisocial as they come. At least that's what I've heard from other cupids.

I follow the reaper to the room, and I'm shocked by what I see.

It isn't a ghoulish reaping of a soul, no; he takes the hand of the old man's soul and pats it with both hands. I can't hear what he's saying, but the old man is smiling, like he's relieved. Like he's welcoming death with open arms. It's actually quite sweet, and I nearly feel like I'm intruding on a special moment.

The machines beep wildly as his soul disappears peacefully; the man crossing over to the afterlife. Then the reaper turns his hooded face toward me, completely unreadable. His body floats closer to stand in front of me. I have to look up, and yet, I can still only see the bottom half of his face.

"What are you doing here, cupid?" he asks, the deep timbre of his voice sending a shiver down my spine.

There's a flurry of humans around us, hoping to resuscitate the older man. Yet, we both know he's gone. There's no coming back after a reaper has collected your soul.

"It's actually quite interesting, if I could have a moment of your time?" I say with a smile. "I promise it's not about your car's extended warranty or a religious cult." I swear his lip twitches, but I can't tell from the overhang of his hood.

"I don't have time for this shit. I'm busy."

"I totally get that you're busy, but it will just take a few moments," I say.

He zooms down the hall, and I snap out my wings to follow him. It's taken me a lot of practice to get used to these wings, popping them in and out is a total bitch, but they come in handy sometimes.

"I know you have an important job... uh... Mr. Reaper man, but I'd like to talk to you about a proposition."

He halts in the hallway and I'm thankful for it as my feet touch the floor and tuck in my wings.

"Are you sure this isn't about a cult? I've never heard of a cupid wanting something from a reaper," he says, pulling his cloak back.

Holy fucking shit, this reaper is hot.

His hair is a dark brown, and it's messy, framing his angular face and complementing his bronzed skin. His eyebrows are just as dark as his hair and highlight his deep-set, brown eyes. He stands nearly a foot and a half taller than me.

I absolutely have to make this work with the reaper. He'd be perfect. He's tall, dark, and handsome. It doesn't hurt that he's also the polar opposite of Eros.

I swallow as I open my mouth, and he glares down at me.

"Don't waste my time, cupid," he says.

"My name is Love. What… what would make this worth your time?" I say.

Clearly, the way I've approached my little problem before didn't work. Perhaps I could trade something so he'll come to the party with me.

He tilts his head at me, looking me up and down.

"What is it that you want?" he asks.

"Could we possibly go somewhere else?" I ask, looking down the sterile hallway.

"Does death scare you, Love?" he asks with a slight smirk.

"No, I just thought somewhere with a little less human activity," I lie.

He holds out his hand, a shadowy mist swirling around his wrist. His cool fingers wrap around mine as he portals us to a park just outside the hospital.

He drops my hand immediately, and it takes me a moment to get my brain back online so I can speak again.

"I'd like for you to attend the Valentine's Day Ball with me, as my date," I say plainly. "I'm willing to trade whatever you want for a few hours of your time."

He tilts his head as he looks down at me, his face unreadable.

"And why on earth would you want to bring a reaper to your little love fest?" he questions.

Honesty is the best policy, at least I fucking hope so.

"Well… my ex broke up with me when he found out I was up for a big award at the ball, and he's bringing his new girlfriend. In a moment of weakness, I may have said that I was bringing a date, and now I really need to show up with a handsome date and win that award so I can rub it in his stupid pink face."

He blinks at me; his face is unreadable, but I swear there's a tick in his jaw. I can't tell if he wants to choke me, make me disappear, or fuck me.

"He's a real dick, my ex. I figured bringing a reaper would really piss him off."

"You're being petty then?" he asks.

"Yes, very much so. Like I said, I'm willing to trade whatever you want," I plead.

"What happens at this party?" he asks, his eyebrow arching.

Okay… maybe honesty isn't the best policy. I don't want to scare him off with what actually goes down. So I keep it simple with my answer.

"Drinks, bacon wrapped scallops, the awards, and dancing," I reply and the reaper looks me up and down.

"Surely there's a cupid that could take you to this party."

"I don't want a cupid," I snap back, putting my hands on my hips.

A smirk takes over his perfectly handsome face as he crosses his arms.

"It sounds like quite the favor. Not only will every cupid be gawking at me all night, but I'll have to actively try to be nice to that lot of love-crazed lunatics."

"You don't have to be nice. In fact, you can be as mean as you want," I reply, truly meaning it. "Especially to Eros."

He hears my ex's name and his dark eyes twinkle for a moment.

"I might be willing to help you, little cupid. But for a price," he says.

"Name it."

There's no fucking way I'm going to this party alone. I need to see Eros' smug face fall as I walk into the party with a super-hot reaper on my arm and collect my award. Surely if the reaper isn't up for the after party, he'll leave, but part of me is sincerely hoping he's down for a little fun.

I've never been with a reaper after all, and he has very large hands and a very broody face. I zone out, thinking about all the things those hands of his could do to me. Things I've wanted but haven't known how to ask for. Someone who can really take control and give me what I want.

He swipes his hand in front of my face and I look up into his dark sexy eyes.

"Three love arrows towards the people of my choosing."

I tilt my head and inspect him.

"That's… not what I was expecting," I reply and he shrugs.

"Three of your love arrows and I'll come to your love fest."

"Deal," I reply, holding out my hand, and the reaper takes it, his larger hand engulfing mine.

"I'm not wearing a suit."

"I wouldn't want you to. You didn't tell me your name," I reply. I want him to come to the party just as he is, every scary hot inch of him.

He smiles, this time truly showing his teeth, and I think I almost pass out with how good he looks. He tugs my hand, forcing me into his space. He doesn't smell like sulfur or anything insidious, instead; he smells like cinnamon and vanilla. He leans down significantly to whisper in my ear.

"I thought it was obvious, little cupid. I'm Death," he nearly purrs it in my ear. "I'll summon you for my arrows."

His body warmth leaves me immediately as he wisps away in a plume of smoke.

This is either the most brilliant or the stupidest thing I've ever done. But either way I can't deny I'm more than eager to fulfill my bargain with Death.

Amore and I are partnered today; we're at one of the local gyms looking for potential love matches. I love trolling for love and lust at the gym—everyone is already worked up, hot and sweaty. I've watched so many people fuck in the locker rooms here. Now that I think of it, a good hot lust filled show might help put me at ease over the impending *reaper meets cupid* ball situation.

"I can't believe you actually convinced a reaper to go with you."

"His name is Death," I say dreamily.

"Daddy Death," Amore jokes, making me blush.

This is what happens when you have a little too much champagne and tell your bestie your deepest fantasies. She knows what she did, but I bypass her comment. Even if I'm currently thinking if Death could fit the bill of having Daddy vibes. A reaper who wants to take charge and dote on me? I think I'd be in heaven… or maybe Hell, I'm not sure.

"He's so hot too, Amore. Like in this dark, broody, sad boy kind of way. I think I'm in love," I tell her jokingly. Maybe not… I'm a love-crazed lunatic just like he said.

"I'm surprised he didn't want more than just three love arrows."

I shrug and watch as the two women on the treadmill try to suss out if the other one is straight or not, it's precious. I give them an extra push by loading a lust arrow into my bow and hitting both of the women, alleviating some of their hesitancy.

They both slow down their treadmills and begin really talking, touching each other's arms and exchanging numbers.

With any luck, they'll be in love and live happily ever after, or at least I'll be able to get a good show in the ladies' locker room this evening.

I smile and turn to Amore, who is also smiling widely.

I might have an absolute vendetta against my stupid ex-boyfriend, but I truly do love love. I mean, it's my name for a reason. I believe in it wholeheartedly, and maybe it's the fact that I so desperately want it for myself that I'm going through all this trouble to show Eros up at the event.

"Good catch." Amore grimaces and looks away towards a couple that's lifting weights together.

"What are you hiding, Amore?" I ask, poking her with my bow.

"It's nothing."

I poke her again and she squeals.

"It's just a rumor. It's stupid. It's not even worth mentioning," she says.

"Tell me." I'm not above tickling her until she spills the secret, and she must see that in my eyes as she relents.

"Eros… he… well, he's been telling people that the only reason you're up for the seductress award is because you were dating him. Everyone knows it's a lie. You use lust arrows like it's your job… I mean, it is your job, but you love lusting the hell out of people."

"That slimy, shrimp-dicked motherfucker." I seethe and Amore's eyes go wide.

"That small?" she gasps.

"That small, and with it being pink and all, I figured it was a good comparison."

"What are you going to do?" Amore asks.

I click my teeth. "I'm going to hit him where it hurts the most."

"In his shrimp-dick?" Amore asks with a laugh.

"No, I'm going to steal his bow."

A grin spreads over Amore's face that matches mine. I consider how exactly I plan on taking his most prized possession.

Cupids don't just leave their bows sitting around willy-nilly. They are coveted and treasured pieces of ourselves. Well, if Eros thinks he can break up with me and make me look like a fool, he has another think coming.

'm not sure why I said yes to the sweet, desperate cupid.

That's a lie.

I hate Eros so much. Any chance I get to mess with that self-righteous prick, I'll take it. Truth be told, I probably would have said yes, anyway.

I'm desperately bored, and Love, well Love is terribly beautiful in a way that isn't suited for a reaper. Yet... she wants to use me for revenge and something about that makes me more endeared to the petty cupid.

She also lied to me about the Valentine's Day Ball, probably so that she wouldn't spook me. But I've been around for a long time, I know exactly what happens at their precious Love New Year, and like I said, I've been without affection for quite some time. A man can only be celibate for so long before he starts to crack, and something tells me the cupid might be down with my particular tastes.

I'm sipping a coffee and reading this week's obituaries when Demise comes to sit next to me.

"How are things?" he asks.

"I'm going to the Cupids' Valentine's Day Ball," I tell him and he hunches over the table, gripping the ends laughing. He's laughing so hard that the black veins around his forehead are pulsating against his bright blond hair.

I roll my eyes at his boisterous laughter and I want to hit him over the head with a coffee mug, but I somehow control myself.

"You've gotta be shittin' me. Clearly you're crashing it? I can just picture you floating over to their cute pink little party and ruining it with your presence."

I take a sip of my coffee as Mors joins the table; she glares at the way Demise is laughing hysterically, I understand the sentiment completely.

"And what, pray tell, is so funny?" she asks, pouring herself a cup and coming to sit at the table.

"Good old Death here is going to the Cupids' Love New Year," Demise says, tears filling his eyes as he continues laughing over the prospect.

Mors, however, tilts her head and looks at me with intrigue.

"A sweet little cupid invited me," I tell them, strangely, in a proud tone. Like it's such a victory to have one of the other immortal beings ask something of me, especially a cupid. Especially Love. She's different from some of the other cupids I've had the misfortune of running into. She wasn't scared of me. If anything, she looked like she wanted to take a peek at what's under my robes.

Mors clicks her tongue and sips her coffee, glaring at me over the rim. It's a black mug with a skeletal hand giving the finger. It's very on brand for the moody reaper.

"Does she know anyone else that needs a date?"

Her question takes me off guard, and I just blink at her for a moment.

"You want to go to their precious little party, Mors?" Demise jokes with her.

She shrugs her shoulders, her cloak simmering with smoke for a second, and she looks away.

I hadn't realized I wasn't the only reaper feeling so lonely. But I shouldn't be surprised. This is a lonely gig. Your job is to collect souls, and it's a fairly busy one. Sure, there are reapers who have been in loving relationships for decades, but not us. The three of us sitting around this table have been alone for a considerable amount of time.

Fuck, we're pathetic.

"Do you really think a cupid is going to be attracted to all the doom and gloom you bring?" Demise teases Mors.

"First of all, I'm nothing like Doom or Gloom, and I'm more than certain I could make any cupid happy. They're honestly in a constant state of happiness anyway. It's not like it would be hard. Plus, I actually know how to make a woman come, unlike someone else I know," Mors gives Demise a once over and goes back to sipping her coffee.

Demise glares at her, but then turns to me.

"So, tell us about your little cupid."

I finish my coffee and place the mug in the dishwasher, because I'm a good co-worker like that, before sorting out my robes and giving them both a smile.

"Perhaps another time."

Love still feels like my little secret, I mean I don't know much about her, but these two assholes don't need to know that I could barely stop staring at her tits or how precious she was when she was rambling on about the party and how badly she wanted me to come.

I groan with that line of thinking. My thoughts about the cupid have turned feral, I seriously need to get laid.

I teleport to Mama Lucia's house, before I summon my precious cupid. She almost immediately pops into existence, a soft pink cloud gently exploding with glitter with her teleport.

She blinks at me, and I have to do my best not to smile at her. It's tragic how much she makes the edge of my lips want to turn up. I can't decide if I hate it or not.

She's small, but curvy. Curves I can't help but notice as she places her hands on her hips, clear irritation over being summoned so suddenly. But the irritation fades as she tosses her long pastel pink hair over her shoulder and gives me a warm smile.

"Death," she says in greeting. I like the seductive way she says my name, and it's clear that any fear she held earlier has slowly started to drift away.

"Love. I'm ready to use my first arrow."

"Where are we?"

"Mama Lucia's house," I say as we walk up the old brick steps and easily pass through her front door. "I've collected many souls from this home. She takes care of the dying with compassion and respect. She, out of everyone, deserves her own happiness," I tell Love.

She looks up at me, her large pink eyes watering.

"Oh, don't look at me like that, little cupid."

She looks at me like I have a heart. I'm not alive, at least not the same way humans are, so nothing beats in my chest... yet... yet her pretty eyes are stirring something inside of me that I thought had long died.

"This is just the sweetest thing I've ever heard. Are you sure you weren't meant to be a cupid?" she jokes.

"Please don't make me regret this," I sigh and she just beams at me like I'm not the embodiment of the afterlife. No, Love looks at me like I'm more than a reaper, and perhaps I like that more than I should.

She makes a zipping gesture with her lips and tosses the imaginary key before following me through the house. Mama Lucia is sitting at the kitchen table, organizing her bills and looking downtrodden.

"Do you have an idea of who to set her up with?" Love asks.

I shake my head. I guess I hadn't thought this part through. I just assumed that Love would be able to help. She's a cupid, it's her job, and if anything I gave her an easy assignment. The human woman known as Mama Lucia is a kind one. She would be easy for a human man to love.

"Hmm. Well, they need to be in the same area as one another, and don't worry, this will only count as one arrow." Love looks over her shoulder and whistles when she sees the bills. "Ideally someone rich too. Christ."

I have to rub a hand over my mouth to not laugh at the cupid's outburst. She glances over at me with a smirk.

There's a knock on the side door. Mama Lucia straightens out her dress and fiddles with her dark hair in the reflection in the glass of a curio cabinet before answering it.

"Mr. Adams, come in."

He's about her age, if maybe not slightly older, and he's wearing a rather nice suit. He walks in, looking shy as he takes in the woman who is caring for his ailing father.

"How is he today?" he asks.

"Today is a good day, Mr. Adams."

"Please, call me Patrick," he replies.

Love is already pulling out an arrow. She's quick, hitting Mr. Adams first. Then she quickly pulls another and hits Mama Lucia.

The result is nearly immediate in the way they look at each other. Like they've been dancing around this idea for so long, not knowing how the other one felt. Love's arrows have simply made the realization clear. They both have feelings for each other, and now nothing stands between them taking the first step.

Mr. Adams cups her face and really looks at her. He looks at her like he has a reason for living, and she returns the look tenfold.

Love is clasping her hands against her chest in awe as she watches the older couple embrace each other.

"Do you like dogs?" she asks and I nod my head as I look down at the precious cupid.

I'm so completely fucked.

"You're not what I thought a reaper would be," Love says, as she lets the dogs run around her form. It's always strange being around humans—earthly beings—but not being able to truly touch anything living.

It's only when we're in our respective realms that we can eat, drink, and fully touch things. That is, besides other beings that are also immortal and in the veil.

"What were you expecting?"

She shrugs and I can tell she really wishes she could touch the pug breathing heavily next to her. He's hideous and sounds like he needs a puppy-sized oxygen tank, but she looks at him like it's adorable.

"Mean, moody, not someone who wants a caretaker to find love."

"Reapers have a bad rep."

"I'm realizing that," she says softly.

"I suppose some of it is self-isolation. Leaning into the fear that people have is easier than trying to change their minds. Not all reapers are the same, but we tend to be desolate creatures."

"Why do you look so human? I mean, cupids are pink, angels are gold, ghosts are, well, ghostly."

"Reapers take the form of whatever planet they're working on. It's less frightening for the souls when we look like them."

She clicks her tongue and looks me up and down—dare I say hungrily.

"So is this your true form?"

I grin at her and smile. "Yes, I don't look like a skeleton or carry around a scythe like the humans depict. I'm not even sure how that shit started. If you see a reaper, you're not coming back to the mortal plane."

"Huh, do reapers have an event like cupids do?" she asks, seriously eyeing up the dog, wishing she could pet it.

"We have an annual feast on Halloween, but other than that, no."

"Well, if you need me to return the favor and need a date..."

"Are you already squeezing me for a second date, Love?"

She gasps and looks at me.

"I was just offering. Plus, I think it would be interesting to see your realm, and how other reapers compare," she replies, and I swear her pink cheeks get even brighter.

"Oh, little cupid, they don't come close," I tell her confidently.

She swallows and looks me up and down. My heart is quickly thawing for the bright-eyed cupid. How long has it been since I've spoken to someone so easily? Since someone stirred something inside of me?

It feels like centuries.

"Are you excited about the party?"

"Yes, especially now." She bites her lip, contemplating something before looking back at me. "I might not have been completely honest about what happens at the party."

I lean down, resting my elbow on the grass. Holding my face in my hand, I smile at her. Fuck, my face is starting to hurt from the foreign sensation of happiness.

"You don't say."

"Wait, you know what really happens?" she scolds.

I click my tongue at her.

"I've been around for a while, Love. Of course, I know what you deviants do after midnight at your little party."

"And you still said yes," she says, confused.

"Oh, little cupid, it was part of the reason I said yes," I reply.

It's been so long since I've been intimate, though I don't tell her that. Being in a room of cupids isn't ideal, but having my hands on Love, if she'll let me, was an added bonus for her silly little revenge.

"I didn't know how reapers felt about sex. Apparently angels are super prudes, and ghosts can't touch," she tells me, and it's clear she's trying to gauge my proclivities.

I nod my head. It's unusual indeed for different veil immortals to intermingle the way we currently are, but maybe it shouldn't be that way. Carrying the weight of helping souls cross over is a heavy one, and yet being around Love somehow is helping me shoulder the burden effortlessly. If all I'm able to do is help her with her revenge against Eros, I'll do it with flying colors.

"Are you interested in finding out, Love?" I ask her, and she nods her head. "Tell me, are you a patient cupid?" I tease.

"I can be," she replies.

She's eager to please… she's perfect.

"Be a good little cupid and perhaps you'll find out at your party."

"Maybe you're not as sweet as I thought, Death." She bites her lip and I smile wider.

My chest warms, and I know there's a soul that needs to be guided to the afterlife.

"I have to get going. See you soon, Love," I say, kissing the warm skin of her cheek and teleporting to the soul in need.

The smile she brought to my face doesn't leave me for the entire day.

t's Valentine's Day Eve and I can't help the sense of hope that fills me. Not just because every shop boasts little pink and red hearts in the window and the humans are expressing their love for one another. Don't get me wrong, I'm totally on team *'you should show your appreciation every day of the year.'*

But the humans? Sometimes they need a little reminder, and that's why we have Valentine's Day. It's also why the cupid presence on this planet is so high.

Humans are sometimes forgetful of how important love truly is. But not right now. I watch with hearts in my own eyes as couples hold hands, gifts are bought, and dinner reservations are set. Ugh, I love it so much it makes my figurative heart patter and my hands twitchy to shoot the whole place up with love and lust arrows.

This Valentine's Day isn't just about the humans I push to find their perfect match. No, this Valentine's Day I feel some hope for myself. I spread so much love around, it's about time I got my own taste, at the minimum at least some dirty, messy lust.

When I first became a cupid and Eros showed me attention, I felt smitten. I thought I was special for attracting the attention of such a highly regarded cupid that I lost myself somewhere along the way.

When I was with Eros, everything was about Eros. I thought

that I was okay with that. That it was okay to make myself smaller because he took up so much space.

I sigh, thinking about it. I'm mad at myself for being so stupid. I've only had a few short interactions with Death, but in those short moments, I've seen a kindness in him that I never saw in Eros. I feel embarrassed that Eros' station and beauty blinded me.

I also feel used and preyed upon by Eros, and I simply can't let that stand. I don't remember my mortal life, what planet I came from or who I was. He took advantage of a fresh, naive cupid and he needs to learn his lesson.

Hence why I'm currently stalking the cupid. He needs to learn that he can't just keep preying upon inexperienced new cupids and continue taking while giving nothing in return. That isn't what love is about. He's giving cupids a predatory name.

Maybe I'm holding more resentment than I realize.

He's alone as he pops over to Cupidale. I quietly teleport to our realm and follow him into the break room. He runs into Aphrodite and, to no surprise, starts talking about himself to the poor cupid who looks bored out of her mind.

He places his special plated quiver full of arrows on the table and turns away, flirting with the disinterested cupid. Poor Aphrodite, the bastard just keeps droning on and on about how he created conversation hearts and how all red Starburst jelly beans were his idea. He's full of shit, there's no way he's that smart.

I take a breath and as quietly as possible, walk behind Eros and wrap my hand around the cross body section of the quiver. Aphrodite sees me, but says nothing, as I snatch the quiver. I give her a thumbs up for being a girl's girl before teleporting back to Earth.

Maybe it's subconscious, maybe I just really wanted to see him, but I wander the halls of the hospital, looking for Death.

He's leaning against a doorframe as I round a corner, a knowing smirk plastered on his handsome face.

"Love? To what do I owe the pleasure?" he drawls.

I swear he draws out pleasure in a tone that would make anyone weak in the knees. I'd like to hear him say it in a more private place, preferably between my legs.

I think I finally understand the human phrase tall, dark, and handsome. Because looking at Death right now has me nearly speechless. How could anyone not see the tremendous beauty these misunderstood immortal beings hold?

"Love?" he questions again, arching a dark brow in my direction.

"Oh," I gasp out laughing at myself. "How do you feel about being an accessory to a small, teeny, tiny crime? Like there wouldn't be a documentary about the crime if I were human, but I could seriously be fined and spend a few hours in a slammer sized crime," I ask him.

His lip twitches in amusement.

"What did you do?" he asks, his voice deep and amused, not at all frustrated or judgmental. Could this reaper get any hotter?

"I may or may not have hypothetically stolen Eros' super special plated quiver and arrows," I say, shrugging my shoulders.

Death laughs, and it makes my smile widen. His eyes crinkle, and he looks so young and carefree at the moment that I have to stop myself from melting into the floor, or worse crawling to my knees and sliding under his robe to see what he's packing in there. My guess is he's huge, and damn, I hope I'm right.

"How long do you plan on holding his *precious* hostage?" Death asks, holding his hand out. I place the quiver in his large hand and he gages the weight.

"I didn't have a specific amount of time in mind, per se. I mean if I had to give a time frame I'd say when he finally feels remorse for being a predatory, narcissistic tool."

"I didn't realize he hurt you this much," Death says, his knuckles whitening as he grips the quiver. "You must have really cared about him."

"I'm not upset we're not together anymore," I reply quickly. It's not a lie and I feel like he knows that in the way he looks at me. I swear I see a sense of relief as well.

"Then why steal his arrows? Why invite me to the party?"

I tilt my head and look at Death. His face is hard to read, but I've seen a similar look in humans. It's when they're too afraid to say what they're really thinking.

"I'm not doing all of this because my heart is in tatters or because I have residual feelings for Eros."

"Then why?" he asks.

"Because he made me look stupid. Because I feel so naïve for ever liking someone like that, for allowing someone to make me feel less than. It's petty, I know; stealing his quiver and wanting to show him up at the ball. Maybe it's ridiculous, but it's making me feel better, making him look as stupid as he made me feel. I was a new cupid with hearts in my eyes and he took that from me, he should hurt the way I hurt," I spew out, feeling insecure and that perhaps Death is reconsidering our deal.

"I'll keep it safe until you decide to give it back," he says, tucking the quiver in his cloak and looking down at me, not with pity but with something indiscernible.

"I can't tell if you're judging me or not." I cross my arms over my chest and puff out my pink feathered wings.

"Not judging. Admiring," he says with a smirk. "How did you steal his quiver? That pink shitlord never puts it down."

I laugh hysterically at the use of shitlord until I can breathe again and look at Death. He's grinning down at me and I wipe my eyes before answering.

"He just put it down at a breakroom table while he was trying to flirt with another cupid. He has a girlfriend, mind you, and yet he was trying to get under Aphrodite's skirt." I take a second to realize he was probably flirting with all the other cupids while we were together and it forms a knot in my stomach.

Death's fingers wrap around my chin, and he lightly squeezes until my gaze meets his.

"Anyone who would stray away from you is a fool," he says softly.

His thumb is gentle against my skin as he rubs my flesh like I'm precious. The feeling goes right to my cupid head and I wonder if this could possibly be more than a single date. Surely he has to feel this straining connection between us?

"I'll keep this safe in my realm until you decide otherwise," he says, trapping the quiver under his cloak.

"Thank you."

"You'll have to teleport me into your realm tomorrow," he changes the subject.

"We can meet here?" I suggest, and he nods his head.

"Is there a dress code?" He smirks, both of us knowing damn well he's going to show up in his standard cloak.

"You're perfect how you are," I tell him, and I mean it honestly and in every way he could imagine.

Death looks at me like I've dumbfounded him. I just smile before teleporting away. I do still have a quota to meet by tomorrow, especially if I want to win that award.

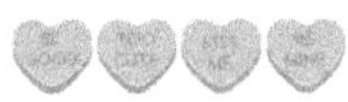

"He has a huge vein bulging in his forehead. Apparently, he's on a manhunt," Amore says, laughing her ass off. "The big wigs are super pissed he lost a plated quiver and are wondering if he's fit to lead on this planet. You're a fucking genius, Love. Truly, this is inspiring."

I smile to myself, shimmying my boobs so that they're front and center in the pink glittery dress I'm wearing.

"He hasn't confronted me about it."

I shrug in the mirror, looking at Amore's reflection. It

honestly irritates me more that he doubts I could be the one to do this to him. Eros clearly thinks very little of me. Well… he's in for the shock of his life tonight.

"Your reaper is still coming tonight?"

"Oh, yes. Once I'm done, I'm going to collect him from Earth and bring him to the party."

"Maybe the vein that's been pulsing on Eros' forehead will explode."

I grin at her in the mirror and waggle my eyebrows; she laughs.

"You're different without him, you know?" Amore says, the joking nature dropping from her face. "He dulled your shine, but now you're brighter than ever. You're going to win that award, roll up with a hot reaper on your arm and show everyone that they've underestimated you. I'm proud of you, Love"

I wrap my arms around the tall, pretty cupid and squeeze.

"I love you Amore," I tell her honestly.

People don't tell their friends they love them enough; it's truly a tragedy. She wraps her arms around me and squeezes me just as tight.

"Love you too, Love."

We part, and she smacks my ass hard.

"Now go get your reaper and show everyone what you're made of."

I nod my head, wink at Amore, and teleport back to the hospital.

It's time to show all these cupids who I really am, a love force not to be reckoned with.

I wait anxiously and pace nervously outside of a patient's room at the hospital.

I'm worried that Love changed her mind. That she realized the push back she'll get for bringing me to the biggest cupid celebration of the year isn't worth the trouble.

She has to know that I won't be fully accepted there, that her choices will be judged. Maybe stealing Eros' most prized possession cured the revenge she wanted out of her system.

She won't need me anymore. The thought is infuriating, and sends a jolt of jealousy and irritation through me. If she doesn't bring me, hell only knows what activities she'll engage in with other cupids. I find myself hating the thought of anyone else's hands on her.

She's a cupid, I'm a reaper, the two don't mix, ever.

Surely, she's come to her senses and just won't show up, realizing that anger blinded her. I'd be more disappointed than I'd ever care to admit.

I've smiled more around the cupid than I have in the last century. I like how she talks rapidly with no filter, how sweet she is while still having a slightly dark side. Frankly, I like everything about the glittery cupid that flew into my life with a sparkling vendetta in her eye. It would be my luck to lose her before ever truly getting to know her.

The time ticks by.

She's nearly five minutes late. The reality of her not showing up hits me and a sadness I haven't felt in a long time consumes me. I was an idiot for thinking that she'd actually show. That she does truly want me there with her. She just wants someone, anyone, to one up Eros.

I'm completely spiraling and hate myself over it. Part of me is mad at Love for digging up these feelings. I was fine before she came along with her soft smiles and precious attitude. Life wasn't complicated, I did my job, did it well, and went home.

Now... now I spend my days wondering if she's floating around the hospital looking for me, if I should summon her, what her lips would feel like on mine. It's simply not very reaper-like. Yet, if the adorable little cupid does show up tonight and bring me to her party, all of these feelings I'm not sure how to process would be worth it.

The patient I'm near has two visitors, they're all talking to each other in low tones. While the tone is jovial, it seems like something is missing. The man in the bed with the broken arm looks at the woman speaking like she hung the moon and she couldn't be more clueless.

I wonder if my fate is the same as the poor bastard clutching his fragile little arm.

At what point would it be considered pathetic for me to still be waiting for Love? I sigh and look up at the ceiling, ready to teleport home when a flash of pink pops before me.

"I'm so sorry, I lost track of time. Are you ready to go?" she says quickly, and I finally get to look at her.

She's always beautiful. But tonight, she's magnificent.

Her long pink hair curls down her back, and the dress she's wearing sparkles and shows off every spectacular curved inch of her body. I have to actively not stare at the breasts she has pushed up high in the dress. Instead, I look at her face, her pretty heart shaped face, and bright pink eyes.

"You look stunning, Love," I tell her and she smiles.

"Thank you, you look handsome," she replies softly.

"Would this be a bad time to ask for my second arrow request?" I ask her and she smiles and shakes her head.

"Valentine's Day is the best day for love matches, you know. Who did you have in mind?" she asks.

I turn my body and hold out my arm to the room.

I don't have to speak as Love assesses the situation.

"It's not unrequited, you know," she tells me, answering a question I didn't ask. "She just needs a little push."

Love opens her purse, pulling out a single arrow, no bow to be seen. She's gentle as she pokes the woman's hip with it. Just like last time, I watch in amazement as something clicks with the woman before us. She looks down at the man who has his arm in a cast and it's almost like it's the first time she truly sees him.

The man notices immediately and smiles at her.

"Amy, do you think after I get discharged we could go out for dinner?" he asks boldly.

"It's Valentine's Day," the woman responds with a breathy voice.

"Yeah, I know," the man replies, his confidence somehow surfacing at this moment.

"Yeah, okay. I think I'd like that very much."

He grins at her, and she leans down and kisses his cheek. The man looks like his world finally makes sense with that one small touch.

When I look over at Love I find her staring at me with a grin on her face.

She holds out her small pink hand to me. There are no words between us, it's almost like she can read the insecurities rolling through me.

It has nothing to do with being in a room full of cupids or her ex-boyfriend. It has everything to do with wanting Love to look at me the same way that girl just did to that broken, hopeless man.

When she laces our fingers together, smiling up at me, for the first time in a very long time I feel a sense of hope. Maybe my life could be something beyond ferrying humans to their final resting place. Maybe, even though I'm not a cupid and haven't believed in love for a very long time, I could find it with this gorgeous little firecracker.

Cupidale is… something.

It's as you would expect, extraordinarily colorful, the temperature is a perfect seventy-two degrees and there's a pink person every direction I look. Though, none of them compare to the cupid currently holding my hand like she would cut off my circulation if I had any. She leads me down a stone path towards a large building, with bright golden lights in front of it.

"If anyone makes you uncomfortable just tell me, and I'll take care of it," she says confidently.

I smirk down at her, the idea of the small cupid defending me easing something in my chest and bringing me a form of pleasure I can't explain.

"You don't think I can take care of myself, Love?" I ask her, leaning down into her space.

"Oh, I think you can more than take care of yourself. But this is my realm; I invited you here as my date. So if anyone is rude to you, I'll handle it."

"What will you do?" I ask, curious and also liking when she comes up with little plots to piss people off. They aren't mean enough to actually cause any damage, but entertaining nonetheless.

"Well, I do have someone who can hide just about anything I'd ask them to in a realm a cupid can't go without an escort." She squeezes my hand, and she's not wrong. If she asked me to hide just about anything for her, I'd do it. "There's also a pet store down the street where you can buy a bucket full of crickets. Would be a shame if someone found their apartment riddled with those pesky things," she says. "There's always the dead fish in an air vent, itching cream, and good ole Saran Wrap over the toilet seat."

"Diabolical."

She smiles at me and gives my hand a squeeze before we enter the party.

Pink and red are everywhere. Every now and then you'll see a touch of gold in the lights and decoration. But between the cupids milling about and the amount of hearts and balloons in the large banquet space, it's primarily the colors of love. I don't find it as sickening as I used to.

This woman is destroying me.

My stark black robes are a severe contrast and the cupids notice immediately. Love holds her head high, as we go to one of the standing tables, it's covered in a bright sparkly red fabric with floating candles as waiters walk around with champagne and appetizers.

"Why do some of the cupids work the event?" I ask her curiously.

She grimaces and shrugs. "Not every cupid passes and gets to work in the field."

"They don't exterminate them?" I reply dryly and she gasps.

"No, they find jobs in Cupidale, paperwork, stuff like that."

"That's benevolent."

"Yeah, us cupids are un-murdery like that. What about reapers?"

I tilt my head and look down at her, plopping a bacon wrapped scallop in my mouth. I won't say it out loud, but it is fucking delicious.

"I've never heard of a reaper unable to do their duties. Come to think of it, it's probably been a solid hundred years or so since someone new joined the ranks."

Her mouth gapes open and she blinks at me.

"How old are you anyway?" she asks and I smile.

"Mmm, old enough."

"To what, party?" she says and I can't help but let out a laugh. This cupid amuses me in a way I haven't experienced before.

She grins up at me and shakes her head. "I like when you smile, and laugh."

"What about when I brood?"

"I won't deny that you have brooding down pat. But you're definitely a softy beneath all those dark shadowy robes," she jokes.

I enter her space, creating a shadow barrier around us and she gasps, looking up at me.

"Do you like shadows, little cupid?" A tendril strokes her cheek, and she shivers.

"I think I just might."

My hand goes up to her cheekbone and I brush it with the back of my knuckles.

"You're so soft."

She swallows and blinks up at me. "Do you like soft?" she asks breathlessly.

"I think I just might."

Our moment is interrupted by the loud playing of harps signifying for us to take our seats.

Love and I stare at each other for a moment before she takes my hand and leads us to a table with the number seven on it. The tablecloth is bright pink—shocker, and the silverware and champagne flutes are gold. There's a hot pink heart-shaped air balloon with a teddy bear in the basket at the center of the table. It's truly obscene.

Cupids whisper and gawk as they walk past us, but Love acts like they don't exist and I attempt to do the same, but mostly I just glare, and keep my mouth shut. Love slides her hand under the table and places a reassuring hand on my thigh. It does nothing to calm my nerves, it just makes my dick hard.

My muscle tenses under her touch and the little pink minx just gives me a smirk, not moving her hand.

Two women come to join our table, one with a look of surprise, another with a look of glee.

"This is my best friend Amore, and her girlfriend Doe," Love greets. "This is my date, Death."

Doe's mouth drops even further, but both the cupids sit.

"You really fucking did it," her friend Amore says blinking at me.

"You were in on Love's little quest?" I ask the cupid who is staring at me in disbelief.

"I suggested it," she swallows.

"Then I suppose thanks are in order," I reply, and Love blushes next to me, I wonder where else I can make her blush.

"I feel like this should count towards my quota," Amore says and Love throws a roll at her friend. "What? It was my idea."

"True, but I convinced him to come," Love says and Amore bursts out laughing, I hide a smirk over the innuendo, and fuck do I hope it comes true tonight.

Love blushes again and squeezes my leg. "Ignore her, and I do appreciate you being my date. I—"

There's a dinging of expensive china interrupting her sentence and all of the cupids take their seats at the rows and rows of tables throughout the space.

The cupid at the podium is near ancient, though you can't tell by appearance. He's young and youthful, but everyone knows he's the oldest thing in this realm, the original cupid, Cupiō.

"Cupids, welcome," he says, while holding his champagne glass in the air. "It's been another year of stupendous love and I'm so honored to have you here today. We're here not to just celebrate your accomplishments, but to also ring in the new year of love. I have a feeling this is going to be the best year yet!" he says happily.

"Before we start with the awards, I'd like to make a toast."

Everyone raises their glasses, except for me. Love squeezes my thigh—hard. I grunt and hold my glass, not nearly as high as the other cupids surrounding me.

"When we love, we always strive to become better than we are. When we strive to become better than we are, everything around us becomes better too."

Did this man, the High Cupid, really just fucking plagiarize *The Alchemist?*

The cupids all smile and toast, and look nearly teary eyed at his toast. Fuck, I really don't belong here.

I down the champagne in one go.

Perhaps I misstepped. Our worlds are so different. Love is filled with glitter and pink and creates people's happiest moments. Mine is dark, gloomy, and I help people in the scariest moment of their lives, no matter how long or short lived.

"With that, let's start the awards," Cupiō says.

Love removes her hand from my thigh to fidget. She's clearly nervous about the award, it's a big deal not only to her but apparently all the other cupids filling the room.

I place my arm over the back of her chair and lazily rub her bare shoulder with my thumb. She doesn't hide her contentment at my touch, so I keep doing it while I lean down to whisper in her ear.

"Win or lose I'll treat you like a winner tonight. But my money's on you."

"Want to make it a bet?"

I smirk, drinking the remainder of her champagne.

"If you win, I'll treat you like the queen that you are."

Her pink eyes blink wildly as she takes me in. She gulps before speaking. "If I lose?"

"Same prize," I grin and she flushes.

She refills her glass with champagne and tosses it back as they go through the awards. Some of them are a little unique, if not borderline stupid, but I don't give a shit about them. I contemplate if there's anything I can do to ensure that she wins. Is there someone I could bribe or threaten?

"Next up is the seductress award," Cupiō announces and Love stills next to me. "This award goes to the cupid who has created the most lust for women on earth." The man is slow with opening the card. "And the winner of the seductress award is Love!"

Everyone claps as she looks on with shock. But then she looks over at me. In the middle of getting her great achievement, *the pretty cupid looks at me.*

Maybe I do have a fucking heart after all, or maybe it's a black hole in my chest stamped with her name.

"Congratulations, Love. Go up there and get your award," I tell her.

She beams at me, leaning over to kiss my cheek. The crowd goes nearly dead silent with the exception of a few gasps. Love ignores them as she goes up to the stage and grabs her big, gold heart trophy and brings it back to the table.

She places it on top of the tablecloth and stares at it.

"I can't believe I won."

"I can," I say softly, and she blinks up at me, a small smile taking over her face. Her pretty light pink eyes shining with unshed tears.

I decide then no matter if Love just wants to be friends and this party is all she wants from me, I'll protect her above all else. But fuck, do I hope she wants more.

*D*eath looks at me like I'm special, and he truly means it when he says he's not surprised I won.

He's proud of me, I realize.

This man who I forced into my life, who barely knows me, is proud of me. Meanwhile, my boyfriend of over a year broke up with me because of this award.

The gold is shiny and perfect. My name is even engraved at the bottom. But when I look over at Death, and how he only smiles at me, I can't help but to think I won so much more than an award.

The last awards are called and Death keeps his arm wrapped around my chair, his thumb grazing my shoulder or playing with my hair the whole time.

Music boasts over the entire hall, and cupids begin loading up the dance floor. *Truly Madly Deeply* by Savage Garden comes on, and Death uses his hand to cover his laugh before clearing his throat and holding out a hand to me.

"Would you like to dance, little cupid?"

"I'd love to," I reply.

His hand is big and warm as it wraps in mine and he walks us to the dance floor. There's a lot of attention on us as the cupids talk about the fact that there's a reaper at our party. He stands out significantly with his height and his dark cloak and hair. I like how we defy odds in our contrast to one another.

He's gentle as one hand wraps around my waist, and he

surprises me by tangling a hand in my hair as we sway to the music. My hands explore his hard, muscular chest, and I hold on to him while the music plays. Damn, I want to explore what's under these thick smokey robes.

It's like we're the only ones on the dance floor. These other cupids cease to exist while I'm in his arms. I didn't feel a fraction of this contentment and warmth when I was with Eros.

Death's hand slides from my hair and cups my face as he looks down at me, his deep, dark eyes soft. He's leaning down to kiss me when an irritating voice ruins the moment.

I press my forehead against Death's chest as Eros speaks.

"Really, Love. Him? That's who you brought to the party. He's killing the mood. I get that I broke your heart and all, but Death, really?"

Death stills, a dark energy radiating off of him. I pat his chest and turn to Eros. A solemn Juliet next to him. For a short moment, I actually feel pity for her, that her date is causing a scene and not enjoying the party with her, but I did do all of this to get under his skin, even if my priorities have shifted.

Eros is nothing in comparison to Death, that's for damn sure.

"He's far better company than who I originally planned on coming with," I say spitefully.

Eros bristles but looks at Death with a look of disgust on his face.

"Death," he says his name with disgust.

"Eros, long time no see," Death replies in a bored tone.

I don't let my surprise show that they know each other, though something sinks in my gut. Did he only say yes because he also has issues with the pompous cupid?

"Not long enough, I'd say," Death adds. He keeps his arm around my shoulder in a possessive way.

Eros clears his throat. "Neither of you would happen to know about my missing quiver."

I suck my lips in my mouth to not laugh in his face.

"I don't know much about a lost quiver, but I do believe your missing balls can be found somewhere in the bottom of the Atlantic Ocean," Death deadpans.

The laugh pours out of me and Eros glares at me before a cruel smile takes over his face.

"No worries, I'm sure it will show up around here somewhere." Eros snaps his fingers. "Oh, Love, darling. I forgot to congratulate you on your award. It's so impressive you won, considering no one else was nominated."

I blink at him, and he smirks.

"Did you think I broke up with you because I was jealous?" He laughs and shakes his head. "No, it's because I was embarrassed."

Death's arm is no longer around me as he grabs Eros by the throat.

Juliet gasps and looks around for help, but Eros smiles in Death's face.

"What? I took your girl a millennium ago, and so you thought you could take mine? Jokes on you because I don't want her."

Eros is waiting for Death to lash out. I can see it in his face. This is what he does. He's a manipulator of mass proportions and he wants a rise out of Death. But he doesn't give it to him. Instead, Death drops Eros like he's disgusting, wipes his hands on his robes and glares down at the irritating cupid.

"I had hoped you'd grown up after all this time, Eros. How absolutely boring of you to stay the same," Death says coldly.

Eros sputters, his ego taking a direct hit. He looks at me with his eyes narrowed, but I'm too busy looking up at Death.

He cups my jaw, his warm hands spanning the sides of my face as he leans down and kisses me. His lips are soft, and the kiss is gentle and smooth. I wrap my hands around his wrists, holding him close to me, before our lips part. His eyes are serious as he speaks.

"You're special. Don't listen to him."

My gaze is so focused on Death that I hardly even notice Eros glaring at us before storming off and throwing a fit in a corner like a child.

"So, you know Eros," I say, feeling slightly insecure.

I mean, I invited him to the party when we didn't know each other. Of course, he had his own reasoning for agreeing to come with me.

"Unfortunately."

"Is that why you agreed to come?"

Death's hand hasn't left my face, and he tilts my chin, forcing me to look at him.

"I'll never lie to you, Love. It was definitely part of the reason I agreed to come with you. But you're the reason I'm still here now," he tells me and I bite my lower lip.

"Who was Eros talking about?" I ask, feeling jealous of someone he dated hundreds of years ago. It's truly not my proudest moment, but I'm a cupid, a petty one at that.

Death's lips twitch, and he shakes his head.

"Honey and I were just friends. It wasn't like that. She needed a way to break up with Eros and I helped her by lying and saying that we were together. It wasn't like this, Love. I promise." He pokes my chest and I feel a glimmer of hope that he's having the same emotional response to me that I'm having to him.

"Like what?" I reply, maybe fishing for compliments or security.

What can I say? Even cupids need reassurances.

He doesn't answer with words, he just presses his lips back to mine. This time, he's more demanding. His hand is tight in my hair as he kisses me passionately. It's hot, rough, and yet I still feel absolutely precious under his touch.

His tongue enters my mouth, and it's back to us being the only people in the room again. Despite the rude interruption, everything around us disappears.

The only two people that matter right now are me and *my reaper*. I quite like the sound of that, *my reaper*. I want to hoard him away and keep him close to me at all times. I'm not sure where this possessiveness is coming from, but something about him brings it out of me.

He's showing me how he feels with this kiss that's speaking louder than words ever could.

It's not just in my head, this easy magnetic-like connection I have with him.

He feels it too. *Right?* There's no way I'm alone in this feeling, not with the way he kisses me like it's his last.

I moan against his mouth and think to myself, *Is there anything better than a new romance?* I doubt it, I feel like I'm on cloud nine.

The butterflies in my stomach are flapping wildly, my nerve endings are on fire, and I never want this kiss to end. I never want this feeling to end. This newness, the chemistry, the way he touches me is everything I could have asked for.

I finally feel how the humans do when I hit them with my arrows, and damn, those fuckers are lucky they have me, because this feels amazing.

Death pulls back, his warm hands still on my skin as he looks down at me. His eyes are a deep pool of brown I want to get lost in.

"Like that, little cupid. It's never been like that."

"For me either," I reassure him. I want to say more; I want to say how happy I am that he's here and this should be more than one night. One single kiss solidified that I need so much more time... so much more everything from him.

Part of me wants to pull his lips back down to mine and kiss him for the rest of the evening, fuck using words, they're over-rated any way. There's also a part of me that wants so much more. I want all his touches, all his sweet words. I want this night to go on forever. It's like we're in a bright, bubble gum pink Valentine's Day bubble that I never want to pop.

The loud speaker comes on.

"One minute until the Love New Year!" it says loudly, but I don't look away from the man in front of me.

He keeps surprising me at every turn. I would have never expected so much from a reaper, and that's mostly because of my ignorance, but I know that no other reaper would be exactly like Death. I've met lady luck before, and I wonder if she had anything to do with me crossing paths with this man.

I can't believe I thought tonight would have been special with Eros, tonight is everything because of the supportive and highly seductive, probably fucking ancient man—reaper—in front of me.

The countdown starts and we just look at each other for a long moment. I wonder if he's thinking all the same crazy things I am. Mostly how I don't want this thing between us to end after tonight.

This all might have started with my loud mouth and wanting to put Eros in his place, but now it's so much more.

I think I'm falling for a reaper.

"Five, four, three, two, one!" the countdown announcer says.

Confetti pops throughout the room, and slowly trickles to the floor along with hundreds of pink and red balloons. It's beautiful, but not nearly as special as the way Death looks at me while cupping my jaw.

The big red heart with gold numbers drops, ringing in a new year of love. His gaze never leaves me, as I take in the Love New Year surrounding us. He swoops down, picking me up and kissing me even more passionately than before.

"Happy Love New Year, little cupid," he says against my lips.

I lick my lips and blink at him. Realizing that cupids are undressing around us. We haven't really talked about what happens after the countdown. I mean, he said he had an idea, but does that mean he actively wants to take part?

Me and my vagina absolutely want him to take part, but only with me. I totally approve of the free-spirited sexual nature of being a cupid, but when it comes to Death, sharing isn't even on the table. I want him to feel possessive of me, and to take care of me, but more than anything I want him to feel comfortable.

"We don't have to stay," I tell him breathlessly.

He looks to our left, where Eros is glaring, an irritated Juliet at his side. I don't even care what they think, but there is a side of me that wants to rub in just exactly how much better off I am.

"Maybe a little show before I hoard you away for my own personal viewing pleasure," he says in his deep voice.

It sends a zip of desire down my spine.

When he falls to his knees in front of me, kneeling before me, I nearly combust on the spot. He rubs his face against my dress-covered thigh, and I gasp in surprise.

"What are you doing?"

"Showing him how you should have been worshiped all this time, what we all know only I can give you. And selfishly, I want to see what your pretty pink cunt tastes like," he says with a smirk.

I don't have a pulse to check, but I think I leave the realm for a moment. Have sexier words ever been spoken? Also the way the word cunt rolls off his lips makes it sound both dirty and precious at the same time. The word is truly underutilized in my humble, cupid opinion.

Death takes his time, grabbing the hem of my dress and slowly pushing it up my legs. He places tender soft kisses up my legs as he inches my dress up my thighs. I have nothing to hold on to, so I just run my fingers through his soft hair and stand there while this reaper is on his knees for me.

I don't think I've ever been more turned on by a sight in my life. For the rest of my eternal life, I'll remember this moment and how reverent it feels. Death looks up at me like I'm a queen and there's no place he'd rather be than having his knees pressed against this confetti-riddled floor, showing me his adoration.

His lips are gentle against my legs as he bunches my dress around my hips and grips the back of my thighs.

Death runs the bridge of his nose along the seam of my panties, taking a deep inhale and licking the fabric, leaving a wet trail in his wake.

I can't keep my eyes off of him. We're back in our Valentine's Day bubble where only we matter, and I never want to leave.

He looks at my pussy with heavy-lidded, lust-filled eyes and I know I'm going to combust as soon as he touches me.

There's moaning all around us, cupids celebrating the Love New Year the way we always do—openly expressing our love for one another. But all that exists for me is this reaper and the unbridled lust between us.

His large hands grip my ass as his fingertips grab the waistband of my panties, and he slowly, nearly torturously, slides them down my legs.

I'm bare from the waist down for him, while he just stares for a moment. A loud guttural moan leaves him, before his lips press against my dripping center and he starts to devour me.

'm sure the cupids who aren't currently lost in their own state of lust are baffled by me on my knees for the tiny cupid in front of me.

But I don't care.

I want them to watch. To see what I see; that Love is wonderful, free, and deserves to be worshiped. They should make a fucking gold-plated statue in her honor and keep it in this ridiculous banquet hall. On the other hand, no, I don't want everyone constantly looking at her.

I really wanted to smash Eros' face in from the moment he interrupted our kiss. When Love's expression faltered while he was attempting to degrade her, I considered murder. He doesn't have a fucking soul, but for the first time in my life I wished I actually had a scythe and could take someone out on my own accord. His only intention was to hurt her feelings, to make her feel less than.

Jokes on him because Love is fucking *everything*.

As much as I want to show Love how perfect she is, I also plan on proving to her that she needs me, that this needs to be more than just one night. There's simply no way I can just leave satisfied after only one night of her, and I've only barely had a taste.

I finally have her bare from the waist down, her pretty pink cunt glistening with shimmery wetness. I can't help but stare for a long moment. It's been far too long since I've been intimate, and looking at her now has me wanting to eat her whole.

So I do.

My arms are tight against the back of her thighs as she stands there, her hands tangled in my hair for purchase as I bring my lips to her sweet pussy.

I'm not sure how to describe Love's taste. All I know is that I'll simply never get enough of it. My tongue lavishes her clit with small circles and flicks. I look up at her from under my lashes, and she's staring down at me with lusty eyes, her pouty pink lips parted in ecstasy.

Fuck, I think I want to see her look at me like that 'til the end of time.

My palms involuntarily squeeze the soft flesh of her thighs as I press her cunt harder against my mouth. Her flavor floods against my tongue and all I can do is moan before using my mouth to make her do it again.

Her thighs are shaking against my touch but I don't want this to end too quickly, so I pull away, kissing her pelvis and thigh, making her huff above me.

She tugs my hair and I look up at her, no doubt there's a sheen of her essence covering the bottom half of my face. I lick my lips and her chest rises and falls as she watches me taste her. I'd spend eternity on this stupid confetti-riddled floor for her.

"That's not very nice," she complains breathlessly.

"I'm a reaper. I'm not supposed to be nice."

"You are to me," she says softly.

I place another kiss on her thigh and drag my teeth against her soft skin.

"That's true. But only for you, little cupid."

She licks her lips and looks around the room before looking back down at me.

"You have quite the audience," she says.

She doesn't sound embarrassed or worried about it. Hell, the cupids are hands-down the biggest freaks in the veil. When your life is endless, there isn't a big fuss about your sexual preferences or kinks. I might hate how joyous they are at times, but based on the sounds around me, these pink misfits know how to fuck.

I kiss her thigh again, and she shivers. My cock is hard and weeping, but I can wait. I want my eyes to be the only ones on her when I fuck her.

"I might fall over if you keep doing that," she jokes.

I'm on my feet faster than she can track, grabbing her by the waist and carrying her to one of the nearest tables. I'm careless as I toss champagne glasses and silverware on the floor. I place her perfect ass on top of the soft table linen, liking the imagery of making a feast out of her.

I block out everyone else in the room. They are irrelevant. My only focus is on Love and how many times I can make her come with my mouth.

Having already kneeled for her, I decide to pull up one of the pink plush chairs and take a seat in front of her.

"Death," she rasps my name. As much as I like my name on her lips, I can think of an honorific I'd like much more. We'll work our way up to that.

The chair screeches, likely drawing more attention as I sit before her, grabbing her thighs and tugging her closer to the table's edge.

"Yes, Love?" I ask with an arch of a brow, my thumb reaching out and strumming her clit.

"Oh, hell."

"Mmm. I go to Hell quite often. This is much closer to Heaven, I'd say."

She knocks over a glass, causing more noise and attention to our table, but falls back on her elbows, still watching me as I toy with her.

"You have the prettiest pussy I've ever seen," I praise her, and her head falls back, her pink gaze blinking at the ceiling.

I slide two fingers inside of her, curling them inwards, hitting that sweet, soft spot. She keens, and her one leg lifts over my shoulder, her heel digging in, directing me where she wants me.

"Bossy cupid," I reprimand her, biting down on her thigh. She only digs her heel harder into my back.

I wonder if my cupid likes her pleasure mixed with a little pain as much as I do. I sure fucking hope she does.

"Please," she begs. It's so soft and sweet.

I need more of it.

I just stare at her, watching her chest rise and fall. Her long pink hair is a mess on the table, and I picture my fist wrapped around the rosy strands as she swallows my cock.

My pace doesn't change, nor do I lick her delectable cunt, even as badly as I want to. I need more of her pleading, her cries as she begs for more… for me.

"Please, Death," she says my name in a moan.

"Please what, Love?" Her name is a soft whisper as I kiss her tender flesh again.

"Make me come. Your mouth, your hands, whatever. Just please."

"And if I were to take my cock out right now and have you gushing all over me that way?" I question, trying to gauge how far she wants this to go. Though I know I won't be fucking her here.

"Yes. I'd want it," she replies confidently.

My dick is hard and aching, but I ignore it as I lean forward and take her clit between my lips and suck. With my fingers fucking in and out of her and my mouth wrapped around her small bundle of nerves, she breaks.

Her nails dig into my scalp, and her leg has me in a fierce grip as she comes undone.

Love's thigh shakes against my face, and her pussy convulses around my fingers. I groan against her wetness, imagining how good she's going to feel wrapped around my cock.

She tugs at my hair, but I don't move, fucking her with my tongue and fingers. She trembles with over stimulation, her ass bucking off the table while also attempting to get away from me.

The gasps that leave her lips become my favorite sound, but eventually I relent. I lick my lips before smearing her release on her inner thigh and look up at her.

"Holy shit," she pants as I slide her off the table and onto my lap.

Her small arms snake around my neck and she toys with the hairs resting on the nape of my neck.

Her gaze looks over my shoulder for a moment, her cheeks flushing before she looks back at me.

"You're so fucking beautiful," I tell her honestly, pushing her soft strands over her shoulder. The heat that flooded her cheeks only gets darker. I want to be the only one to make her blush ever again.

I'm truly fucked over this short, pink woman.

Love's soft hand cups my jaw and her thumb drags from the bottom of my chin to my lower lip before sliding into my mouth. I suck and she sighs dreamily, her eyes flipping from my mouth to my eyes.

"You're not so bad yourself."

"Was Eros watching?" I ask, feeling uncomfortable with the comment.

"I don't care. But hopefully he was and learned a thing or two." Masculine pride fills me that she was too focused on me and her pleasure to care about that fucker, but curiosity and maybe a hit of jealousy gets the best of me.

"What did you even see in him?" I ask.

She shrugs and makes herself small. I hate myself for asking, for ruining the blissful moment we just had. Why can't I allow myself to have anything nice?

"I was a new cupid, all my mortal memories gone, and he was the first person to want to get to know me, or at least I thought so. I was in a new place, and he was this larger-than-life figure. I trusted him and I shouldn't have. It took me a while to warm up to Cupidale and my duties here, but now that I have, I think I have a better grasp on who I am. Being a cupid makes you feel like love is the end all be all, and Eros was that personified. I stayed because I wanted that feeling so bad, but I'm realizing I was looking in all the wrong places," she says, looking at me with a strange amount of softness.

"How much longer do we need to stay?" I ask, wanting to teleport her back to my place or hers as soon as we physically can.

"Let me just grab my award and we can go," she says with a smile.

"We're on the same page that we're leaving here and going somewhere else together, right?" I ask. I leave out the fact that I mean this for more than one night, but nervousness holds me back.

She grins and gets up from my lap, placing a soft kiss at the corner of my mouth before straightening her dress and going to grab her award.

I finally get a serious glimpse of what everyone else is doing. I was so consumed by Love that I didn't really look around. But now that I am, holy fuck.

There's a cupid who's tied up and being fed one cock after another. There's another splayed on a table, each orifice and hand dutifully keeping busy. Then there's the guy taking a fis—.

"There you are," a feminine voice says, not one I'm familiar with.

When I look over at the cupid, I realize she's the one that was following Eros around like a poor, lost puppy. She's pretty, but doesn't hold a candle to Love.

"Sorry, do I know you?"

"I'm Juliet," she says, holding out her hand, which I do not take. Not only because I know she has malicious intentions, but my hand is covered in Love's essence, and that's not something I particularly care to share. It's mine. I'm the one who wrung it out of her perfect body, I'm not sharing.

She pulls her hand away and laughs. "So, you're like the first reaper that's ever come to the Valentine's Day Ball. I was wondering if you would like to dance," she says boldly.

There's suddenly a loud clunk against me as Love slams her heavy award down on the table. She looks pissed and I want to fall to my knees all over again.

"I've tried to be nice to you, Juliet. I've taken pity on you, knowing what you have to deal with when it comes to Eros." Love holds up her thumb and pointer finger, squeezing them tight together and narrowing her eyes. I have to hold back a laugh that she's diminishing his manhood. "But if you think I'm going to let you come over here and try to flirt with my man, you've got another thing coming."

My chest puffs out against my own will. *Her man.* I like that.

Juliet begins to sob, and Love's tone completely changes as she approaches the younger cupid.

"I just wanted him to notice me, you know? He was so upset when you brought him," Juliet says, waving a hand in my direction. "This whole friggin' night all he's been able to talk about is you and your reaper. I thought… I thought that maybe he would get jealous and give me attention if I spoke to him."

"Oh, stupid cupid." Love sighs and hugs the other woman. "Eros is a narcissist. He's mad because I embarrassed him. I bruised his ego. You could do so much better than him. I know he seems larger-than-life at first, but I promise he's not."

"He made me feel like I was special."

Love sighs and looks at me, and I wonder if she's thinking about my words from earlier, about when I told her she was special.

"I can tell you this with one-hundred-percent honesty. You'll find someone better," Love says to Juliet.

"You think so?"

"I know so. In fact, take a look around. Join any of the groups here and you'll have a better experience than with him. Don't let him ruin your Love New Year," Love says.

Juliet sniffles and hugs Love. It's no wonder this cupid has me under her spell, she's simply just a wonderful person. *One you don't deserve*, a dark voice in the back of my head seethes.

"I'm really sorry for acting like that and coming over here to flirt with you," she says to me and to Love.

Love shrugs. "That pig-headed douche will make you do desperate things, I get it."

Juliet smiles and walks away, and Love turns to me, grabbing her award.

"I thought you were going to hit her with it," I joke and she smirks.

"It wasn't so long ago that I was in her shoes. She'll figure it out. But violence is never truly off the table," she says, wiggling her eyebrows and clutching her award like a weapon. "Your place or mine?" she asks seductively.

"Yours," I reply and she grabs me by my robes, teleporting us away.

There's a brief moment when I feel nervous about showing Death my apartment. But it fades away as soon as we're at the edge of my bed.

He isn't focusing on the amount of Valentine's themed stuffed animals or raising a brow at my deep-red, silk sheets. No, the reaper only has his eyes on one thing—me.

His gaze doesn't leave mine as he walks me back towards the bed. He's a man with one singular focus, and for the love of Hallmark, it's nice to be the center of someone's attention.

My attraction to the man in front of me is beyond just how hot he is. Like the stupid cupid I am, I'm falling fast.

He's kind, loyal, supportive, and, well, he can eat pussy like no other. How would anyone expect me not to catch extraordinarily big feelings for this man? Part of me wants to ask what we are. Does he have hearts in his eyes too, or does he just want this one night?

Please don't break my heart, Mr. Reaper.

I'm a cupid, I'm on the hunt for the next fix of love in my everyday life. Am I possibly overthinking all of this? Looking for love in places it doesn't belong? I sure fucking hope not.

"Shut up," Death rasps.

"I didn't say anything."

"It's like you have an evidence board above your head and you're trying to connect the dots. What would quiet that pretty little head of yours?" he asks.

His fingers trail along my jawline until he applies pressure to my bottom lip.

If he doesn't have hearts in his eyes at this moment, a blow job will certainly put them there.

I tug on his dark robe.

"Does this come off?" I ask, and he smirks at me, snapping his fingers and the garment disappears. Okay, that was extremely attractive.

I'm left stunned by his nearly naked form in front of me. His muscles are firm and strong, covered in black and gray tattoos. He has the perfectly trimmed v that leads to what is undoubtedly a massive dick behind his black briefs. It's like an arrow pointing down to my delicious surprise.

But his thighs… his thighs are huge and I want to sink my nails into them or maybe my teeth.

He's beautiful in a way I'm not sure how to describe. The dark edge he carries only adds to his allure. If tonight is all I get, then I plan on taking full advantage. But for the love of expensive floral bouquets I sure hope it's not just for one night.

My dress protests, but I slide off the bed and fall to my knees before him, just like he did for me at the party. He is also certainly deserving of worship, and I plan on making that evident in the way I touch him.

His hands are loose at his sides as I grip the waistband of his briefs and tug them down. His large cock springs free, nearly slapping me in the face. I push them down to his ankles and he kicks the offensive material away. He's completely naked and gorgeous in front of me.

Is it pathetic that I know I'm going to live forever and nothing will ever come close to this? No cupid will hold a candle to his perfect combination of dark and sweet. I almost want to laugh over the fact that I'm calling a reaper named Death 'sweet,' but it's beyond fitting.

I stroke his shaft twice, and lick the weeping tip with my tongue, looking up at him for approval.

Death's fist wraps tightly around my long hair, tugging the strands at my scalp with just the right amount of pain.

"And here I thought you couldn't get any prettier, Love."

I part my lips and slide him down my throat, my gaze not leaving his, even as my eyes water and he presses my face closer to his pelvis.

My nose touches the neatly trimmed hair at his pubic bone, and he groans. His fist is tight in my hair as his head falls back.

"Look at you taking it all. Such a good little cupid, aren't you?"

I nod as well as I can with him down my throat, and he smiles down at me. Fuck, he's perfect.

He pulls my head back and I take a gasping breath as a trail of spit connects the tip of his dick to my bottom lip. My tongue strikes out, breaking the chain, and it falls down my chin.

I grip his strong, manly thighs and take him down my throat again. He continues holding my hair, but lets me control the pace as I lick the crown and length of him. He moans loudly when I cup his balls and my fingers massage his perineum while I suck lightly on the head.

"Fuck, Love."

I hum around his cock and don't stop. His hips move back and forth, pressing in and out of my mouth, while he watches me like I'm the most fascinating thing he's ever seen. I might be on my knees for him, but this feels like it's for the both of us. Wanting to bring Death pleasure is almost as natural as breathing.

"Take the dress off," he demands.

I pop my mouth off of him and stand and turn my back to him, so he can help me unzip.

He moves torturously slow, kissing my bare shoulder repeatedly as his deft hand slowly tugs the zipper down. Death's knuckles drag along my back, leaving goosebumps in their wake.

"Did I tell you how beautiful you looked tonight?" he asks, a whisper against the shell of my ear that has me shivering.

"You might've mentioned it."

"I meant it. I haven't been able to keep my eyes off of you all night."

My body is on fire. It feels so good to be complimented, to be treated like a prize instead of an accessory. The emotions I'm feeling towards him are like a sharp slap to the face, but I don't care. Maybe I stepped on a love arrow and forgot about it, but I can't deny this connection between us.

Death finishes with the zipper, still placing kisses along my shoulder blades and the side of my throat. If you had told me that a reaper would be a sensual and giving lover a few days ago, I would have laughed in your face.

But at this moment? With his tender kisses and his complete focus on me, I can't imagine anything other than complete adoration from the man who stands behind me.

My dress puddles to the floor and I push it to the side. I'm braless and Death takes notice immediately. Wrapping his arms around me, he holds a breast in each hand while his thumbs rub soft circles against my peaked nipples.

"These fucking tits." He groans against my neck.

His tongue swipes against the sensitive flesh of my throat, before his lips suck, no doubt leaving a dark pink bruise in his wake.

His hard cock is rubbing against the cleft of my ass as he fondles me, slowly exploring my body.

"I need to have your sweet little pussy first, but I need to fuck these at some point." He moans behind me.

He pushes my breasts together and squeezes. Of course, my stupid romantic heart skipped past the titty fucking part and went directly to him saying *at some point*. That totally insinuates this is more than a one-night thing, right?

"I don't even know where to start with you." He sighs.

One of his hands frees my breast and slides ever so slowly down my torso until he's cupping my pussy.

His two fingers slide over my entrance and clit lazily as he breathes into my ear.

"I plan on having you as many times as I can tonight. How do you want it, Love? Do you want it sweet?" he asks, pressing soft kisses on my shoulder. His fingers slowly circle my clit, reiterating what he means by sweet. "Or do you want me rough?"

His hand leaves my pussy for a short moment, only for it to whoosh in the air and strike my pussy. It wasn't hard, but it's enough to make me gasp with a jolt of need.

"I'll give you whatever you want, Love. All you have to do is ask, and I'll give my girl whatever she needs."

His girl.

I think I come on the spot.

"Rough," I grate out, knowing that if he makes love to me and is super sweet, I'll simply perish and never return. It would be so embarrassing if he had to collect my soul after making sweet precious love to me.

His hand leaves my pussy as he smacks my ass. The crack of his hand meeting flesh is intoxicating as I take in a breath and wait for another. He doesn't disappoint as he spanks me again. Death grips my hips and our bodies are flush, his front to my back as he whispers in my ear.

"You'll tell me if it's ever too much?"

I nod, and he smacks my ass again.

"Words, Love."

"Yes, I promise."

"Good. Now let's see how many times I can make you come."

He grabs me by the waist, tossing me on the bed. My hands automatically come up, and I catch myself before my face hits the mattress. Death tugs my legs wide so that my ass is in the air, my pussy on complete display.

He smacks my right cheek three times, making me moan and fist the sheets beneath me. He kneads the flesh and laughs.

"Look at that dark pink," he groans.

His teeth slide against where he smacked me and he bites down, making me gasp and attempt to slide away.

"None of that," he scolds.

He parts my cheeks and before I can even speak, he's devouring me. He leaves no inch of me untouched by his devious tongue—and I mean every inch.

"Please, I need you inside of me," I beg.

He laughs, his tongue rimming my tight hole, and his palm strikes my already tender ass. I moan, the mix of slight pain alongside the sensation of him bringing me pleasure. It's the perfect combination of soft and hard… just like us.

"Be a good little cupid and do as you're told, and then I'll give you my cock. Fuck, look at you, dripping all over the mattress. Such a needy girl." He ends his sentence with a harsh slap and I suck my lips in my teeth and attempt to shift my body and find some friction.

"Make yourself come and I'll give you my cock," he suggests.

I go to turn around, but he stops me.

"Oh no, I want to watch with this view. Your pussy dripping, your tits swaying each time you fuck yourself. Let me see it, Love."

I don't need further instruction. My goal is clear, come as fast and hard as I can and then this infuriating man will give me what I want. Gods, do I need him inside of me, I need everything he's willing to give.

I can feel his gaze on me, and I swear I can hear him stroking himself. The idea of him touching himself while watching me spurs me on even more as I slide my hand between my legs and touch myself the way I like. With three fingers, I circle my clit quickly, wanting so badly for him to touch me again. There's so much pressure and I usually use my toys to get myself off, but I'm absolutely determined.

"Do you ever fuck yourself with your fingers?" he asks, his deep voice nearly startling.

"I have toys for that," I pant.

"Where?"

"Nightstand."

My face is pressed against the direction of the nightstand, which is great because I get a gratuitous view of Death's hard cock as he walks by. He's confident as he opens the drawer and clicks his tongue.

"Naughty little cupid."

I shrug and continue fingering myself as he shuffles through my hoard of toys, taking each of them out one by one with fascination.

"Saving these for later," he says, pulling out the cherry red heart-shaped nipple clamps and placing them on the tabletop. "This too." The loud metal clank of the butt plug with a heart-shaped base follows. "Cute," he says with a laugh, pulling out the white silicone toy that's covered in hearts.

He shuts the drawer, leaving the clamps and plug on the nightstand, a reminder of what I'm in for tonight. *I can't fucking wait.*

My hands continue circling my clit as he places the toy in front of my face.

"Get it wet, Love."

My pussy clenches and I open my mouth, taking the toy between my lips as Death watches me with rapt focus. His fingers push my hair off my neck and caress my jaw before he removes the toy and walks behind me.

The toy presses against my entrance slowly, too slowly.

I make a petulant noise and he laughs.

Maybe the reaper isn't as nice as I thought after all. But then again, maybe I truly never wanted nice.

He pushes it deeper inside of me and I can feel his breath against my backside. He's watching me take every single inch as I touch myself. Something about him being so turned on by just watching does something to me. The added stretch of the dildo is exactly what I need, and I pick up the speed against my clit.

"Good girl," Death murmurs with a light smack to my ass, and I fall apart.

I clench against the toy and pant against the sheets as I find my release. He's relentless with the toy even as I ride out my high and I'm shivering.

He doesn't even give me a moment, before I'm flipped around on my back and he's sliding into me with a rough thrust.

lose control watching her pussy milk the ridiculous toy with hearts all over it. I remove the dildo from her sweet cunt; it glistens with her release as I toss it on the floor and flip the little cupid on her back.

As much as I want to fuck her so hard from behind and watch her ass bounce around my dick, I equally want to look into her pretty pink eyes while I make her shatter beneath me.

Her body is still convulsing as I press myself deeply inside her with no preamble. At least I'm bigger than the toy. Could you imagine being shown up by a piece of plastic with hearts all over it?

Her knees press against her chest as I slide my hands in her hair and hold her face as I fuck her.

Love's pretty tits bounce with each thrust, and I'm fascinated with each press of our bodies. I can't help but lean down and take her nipple in my mouth. She moans and tugs on my hair in return.

I fucking love it.

I suck harder, and her back arches against my face and her head pushes me down. I pull sharply, and she gasps as I let the bud free and reach over to the nightstand. My gaze meets with her pretty pink one for confirmation. She sucks in her bottom lip and nods.

"Made for me," I whisper, not knowing if she hears.

I reach for the nightstand without pulling out of her and grab the clamps. My dick is pressed deep inside of her warm pussy, and I feel like I could come just from staying still inside of her.

But I resist, and use my thumbs to make sure her nipples are nice and hard.

I put one of the clamps between my teeth as I use my fingers to loosen the two sides and place them on her left nipple before tightening. I have to stop myself from laughing and choking on the damn clamp when I realize the middle piece is made to look like a Cupid's arrow.

"Fucking cute," I mumble around the jewelry in my mouth.

When she moans and bites down on her lip, I know it's tight enough before moving to the other. I place the other one on her other nipple and her pussy clenches around my length. She grips a heart shaped pillow that says *be mine* on it, and I grin.

I take a breast in each hand, squeezing and admiring how fucking full and perfect they are. The red hearts pressed against her nipples only adding to how attractive she looks splayed out for me.

"Goddamn, baby."

She moans and her legs wrap around my lower back and she pulls me in closer, taking me even deeper than before.

I tug lightly on the clamp and she pants, audible puffs of air leaving her as she moans.

My hips snap, and her perfectly clamped tits heave with each thrust.

I wrap my hand around the back of her thigh, pressing her knee into the mattress and she keens.

"Right there, oh fuck," she moans.

I'm relentless as I pound into her, needing desperately to fill her up and claim her as mine. She needs to understand that she belongs to me, I need to fuck her so good that she's convinced. Every inch of her pretty pink body belongs to me now.

"That's it. Look at you, milking a reaper's cock."

It breaks her, her pussy spasms against my cock, and I'm quick with two fingers, releasing one of the clamps and tugging it off.

It has her screaming as her cum drips down my shaft and over my thighs. A few tears trail down her face with her release and I kiss them as I fuck her harder through her peak.

She writhes beneath me, her body trembling, but she takes what I give her. Our flesh smacks audibly throughout the room until it finally hits me. My much-needed release shivers down my spine, and I moan into her hair as I fall on top of her and fill her with my cum.

Her breaths are raspy underneath me, but she doesn't ask me to move. She draws patterns on my back as we lie there, both of us catching our breaths after what is single-handedly the best sex I've ever had in my life.

Her heart is beating rapidly against my chest and it's only now that I look around her room. It looks like Valentine's Day threw up in here, but I can't say that I hate it.

I pull back and push her hair off of her face and look down at her hazy eyes.

"Okay?" I ask, checking in with her.

She licks her lips and nods. "More than okay, Death... that was..." She seems lost for words, and I'm not sure what to say either.

"It was perfect," I say, not knowing any other words that can truly meet what that was for me. I wish I were better at expressing how I feel. I wish I could just spew out that it was the best sex I've ever had and it's only the tip of the iceberg.

Love trusted me, with her body, with her pleasure, and she did it with no fear. This pretty, lively, lovable cupid trusts me—a fucking grim reaper. It shouldn't be possible, but I crave her bubbly, loving nature more than I've ever wanted anything. I want all of her, every precious, heart-shaped piece of her.

Speaking of heart-shaped, I look down at her nipple.

"Can I?"

She nods and I'm gentle as I unfasten the metal and it releases her. She gasps, and I lean forward and place a tender kiss against the soft bud. Love's nails scratch lightly against my scalp, and I look up at her as she pushes some dark hair out of my face.

Maybe I'm reading too much into it, but it feels like the cupid is looking at me like she wants the same things that I do. Would she risk her standing as a cupid? Sure, she brought me to the party to make a statement, but to really be with me would be to break away from societal norms.

"You're beautiful too, you know?" she whispers.

I shake my head, and she pushes more hair out of my face.

"You weren't what I expected. You are so much more," she says, and I swear it feels like she shoved one of her arrows into my chest, my heart aches and I want to spill my guts to her, but I don't.

Fear holds me back.

Fear of rejection, and going back to my life the way it was before this stunning pink creature entered my life.

"Stay?" she asks, and I nod my head. Does she mean the night or forever? I want her to mean forever.

I hiss when I pull out of her and then pull back, watching as my release spills out of her and onto the silky red sheets.

"That can be your side of the bed then," she says with a laugh and walks over to the bathroom. I follow her like the hopeless puppy that I am as she turns on the spray.

I fuck her nice and slow against the wall of the shower and wonder how in the fuck I got so lucky.

Maybe I don't hate Valentine's Day anymore.

It's been about an hour since we got out of the shower, and we lie on Love's bed. She's completely passed out, her lips parted as she breathes heavy with sleep, her face pressed against my chest.

Has anything ever felt this good? *No.*

I, of course, don't remember my mortal life, but I can't imagine anything that comes close to how I feel right now. For the first time in a long time, I feel like I'm more than just a reaper, I'm more than just my job.

Love makes me want things that I haven't considered in a very long time. I want to protect her, dominate her, own her, and maybe… just fucking maybe she wants that too.

Perhaps there's more to my immortal existence that I ever took into account—love—both in the emotional sense, and the sleeping woman on top of me.

Neither of us have said a word about what happens after this. Our deal was for me to come to this party to show up Eros, but could she possibly want more?

Could this sweet, hopeless romantic find it in her heart to want me, a reaper with a dark cloud following him?

I think she could.

My lips press against her hair, and I inhale her strawberry scent and groan, my cock hardening even though I was just inside of her not even an hour ago.

There's a warmth in my chest that I don't know how to discern, but then I realize I'm being summoned to collect a soul.

"Love?" I whisper her name, not wanting to wake her up. I kiss the side of her face and dress in a flash.

"Love?" I say her name with a little shake; she snores lightly and turns to her side, her pink hair spilling over the pillows. "I'll be back later," I tell her with a kiss to the side of her head.

There's nothing around to leave a note, so instead I grab one of the heart-shaped nipple clamps, hoping the cupid will realize I'm wanting to hear from her as soon as possible. If I get this done quickly, I can come right back into her warm bed before she even wakes up.

I teleport to Earth and realize that while I can pop out of Cupidale, I can't pop back in.

Shit.

I'll just have to summon Love as soon as I have the opportunity. I know all the cupids have the day off tomorrow, but as soon as she's back on this plane, I can summon her and ask her out on a proper date. I can tell her that I don't want this to just be one night, that despite all the odds, I'm falling for the darling cupid.

I twiddle the metallic heart-shaped clamp and place it in my pocket, a smile on my face as I go about my job, ferrying souls to their afterlife. I never hated my job, it can be heavy at times, but knowing Love will be back in my arms, I find even more compassion in what I do as I collect the soul crossing the veil to the afterlife.

wake up alone and a sense of sadness falls over me.

Did he really just leave? No goodbye, no thanks for the transcendent sex that will haunt me for the rest of the sexual encounters I have in my very long existence?

I thought when he looked at me last night he was having the same thoughts I was. Even in his dark gaze, I could have sworn I saw hearts in the reaper's eyes.

I'm so fucking stupid.

Why am I like this? I love the idea of love so much that I fall too hard, too fast, and it's always unrequited. Eros loved himself too much and Death… I don't know what Death wanted from me, just my body?

My eyes sting, and a glittery silver teardrop falls down my eye. I wipe it away angrily and turn the lamp on by the side of my bed. The unused butt plug mocks me, the heart-shaped gem at the end glinting at me with distaste. There's only one nipple clamp on the nightstand and I curse. It probably got tossed somewhere around the room last night.

Great, the reaper ditched me and I have a missing nipple clamp in this room. I have too many fucking pillows on my bed, I'll never find it.

I should have said something. Maybe if I said that he caused butterflies to flap around in my stomach, and that I like his company, he would know where I stood and he wouldn't have brought me back here—he wouldn't have made me like him more.

I'm such a stupid fucking cupid.

Of course, a reaper wouldn't want to settle down with a frantic cupid who never shuts up. I just wish… well, I just wish he would have said something to me instead of sneaking out in the middle of the night.

Maybe if I prepared myself for a one-night stand, I wouldn't feel so torn up. That's a lie, my dumb heart was invested way before we got to that party. How could I get my signals so screwed up? The way he kissed me, the way he devoured me, that isn't normal for just a casual encounter.

My bright golden heart award glistens on my dresser, and I sigh. It's like emotional whiplash, last night being one of the best in my existence, to now feeling lower than low.

How can I constantly be so wrong about men? I'm supposed to be a fucking cupid for Christ's sake. I should be able to spot my own match a mile away. I thought that maybe Death could have been that for me. Cupids love bringing up how opposites attract all the time, most of our job is bringing them together.

But yet, here I am, alone. This Love New Year is starting off really shitty.

It gets even worse as a pink letter pops open right in front of me.

Oh, fuck. A summons, and not the kind I wanted.

Dear Love,

You have been formally summoned to the board of directors office to discuss current behaviors and to discuss your performance as a cupid. You are expected at the High Cupid's office in forty minutes.

Thank you,

Secretary to High Cupid, Cupiō, Ladybird.

Awesome, spectacular. Not only am I in a spiral of self-pity, I now need to have a personal visit with the High Cupid himself, and on the Love New Year. February 15th is supposed to be the day we all get to take a fucking breather, but I guess not.

I brush my hair and dress, knowing I'm walking to my demotion, if not something even more sinister.

Ladybird is a crotchety bitch of a cupid, she glares down her glasses at me like I'm dog shit she stepped in.

"High Cupid will see you now," she drones.

I just nod my head and take a breath before stepping into his office.

"Ah, Love. Please take a seat," Cupiō asks. To be honest, he's a great High Cupid, but nothing about this situation puts me at ease. "Congratulations on your award, it's much deserved."

"Thank you, sir."

"You had an interesting choice for a date. The first non-cupid ever invited to the Valentine's Day Ball, I'm assuming you know this caused a bit of a stir."

"I'm sure it did, sir."

The High Cupid smirks into his coffee cup and looks up at me.

"I'd never try to break up a true love match," he says, and I blink at him. A true love match? Is he high? Because Death absolutely fucking dined and dashed on me this morning. "In fact, I think more cupids could follow your lead and welcome other members of the veil to our world."

"Really?" I ask, my tone filled with surprise. I totally thought I was being fired, not getting kudos for bringing a reaper to the party. A reaper who I'm trying really hard not to think about or else I'll cry a river.

"Yes, our lives are incredibly long. How boring to not branch out. Though, there's something we need to discuss."

I nod my head and my heart stops racing for just a beat. At least I'm not getting the axe.

"You need to return Eros' quiver," he states, and I open my mouth to reply, but he cuts me off with a swipe of his hand. Well shit, I guess there's no lying about that. "I know you took it, and I know my son is a piece of fucking work and I'm to blame. But if you could please return the quiver, all will be set right. My son and I have already had a discussion on how we treat others. He's been sent to the Hoxorian planet to work through his issues."

My eyebrows rise and I'm jealous for a minute and then I remember some of the kinky stuff they're into on that planet. Oviposition is big there, and I mean, I could totally see the allure of it, but it has to get old after a while… right? Maybe not, maybe I should ask for a day pass to just check it out. I feel like it's something you should see at least once.

Cupiō taps his desk, forcing me to pay attention to him.

"Return the quiver and he'll be on his way."

"Yes, sir."

"I'm hoping we'll see your reaper for May Day," he says, and I just nod my head even though my heart aches.

Great, now I have to track down Death to collect Eros' fucking quiver. Swallowing my pride to get it back will not be easy. What am I supposed to do? Troll the hospital, wait for him to show up and say, hey, you lay the best pipe I've ever had and oh yeah, I'm falling in love with you and you feel nothing in return and then sob into his dark robes while he looks at me with disgust?

The thought alone has me shivering and wanting to put my own arrow through my neck so I don't have to live through the firsthand embarrassment.

"Of course, I'll get the quiver returned right away."

"Lovely, looking forward to seeing more of you and your reaper, Love."

I nod my head and leave his office. Ladybird scowls at me and a dark part of me wants to give her double middle fingers and tell her to fuck herself, but that would be very un-cupid like, and I'm already on thin ice.

I bite the bullet and teleport to the hospital, hoping my ego doesn't take too much of a beating in the process.

I hate the hospital, hate it even more that I'm about to run into Death and feel a yearning desire while he feels… more than likely nothing.

Maybe I was wrong about the reaper. Maybe he's not as soft and gooey on the inside as I first thought. Maybe reapers are all a bunch of assholes who fuck you so good they rock around your brain cells too hard and make you forget all your bad bitch morals.

I thought my breakup with Eros was the start of a new era. You know? I thought I was swiftly in my Reputation Era moving to my Lovers Era. The queen of Earth would be so disappointed to see me looking absolutely pathetic right now. I tuck my pink wings tightly behind me as I roam the halls and look for the guy I was falling for.

I hate being a stupid cupid.

Played for a fool twice in such a short span of time is embarrassing. They should clip my wings and crack my arrows in half, 'cause clearly I don't know shit about love.

There's a piece of black fabric swinging into a room and I sigh heavily as I follow it inside.

It's Death, and he's gentle with the soul. I can hear him assuring the old woman about where she's going, and she looks at peace.

Why does he have to be so good at his job and so kind to the humans he transports to their final resting place? And what is it about me that's so disposable? That one night was all he needed? That no one wants to stay with me long enough to truly get to know me sinks into my bones and I'm afraid I might break.

My stomach sinks and my eyes well up with tears.

Fuck.

I'll ask Amore to come by and get the arrow back. I can't face this right now. My pathetic little heart feels crushed. I didn't feel a fraction of loss when Eros broke up with me, but right now, I feel like someone kicked me right in the chest.

I'm about to teleport out when Death's large hand wraps around my upper arm. "Love, there you are. I thought cupids always had the fifteenth off," he says.

"Hi," I reply meekly, and he tilts his head at me.

"Is everything all right?"

No. You hit it and quit it, breaking my fragile, stupid heart in the process.

"Just in a wee bit of trouble with the High Cupid. I need to return Eros' quiver."

"Does this have anything to do with me?"

"No, but I need to return it as soon as possible, so I don't get reprimanded," my voice is soft, pathetic even.

He blinks at me, and a confused expression takes over his face.

"Is there anything else?"

Great, he wants me out of his hair as quickly as immortally possible. If I didn't need that quiver I would have rotted all day long in my stupid stained sheets. My self-esteem is in tatters, and I'm starting to loathe Valentine's Day.

That thought nearly makes me gasp. I'm truly going through it right now.

"No, there's nothing else," I reply flatly.

"Right… I'll go get it and be right back. There's nothing else you wanted to talk about?" His voice is flat, edging on irritation.

"No."

He inhales deeply through his nose like he's frustrated, probably from me stalking him and that he couldn't make a clean break. He shakes his head and sighs, teleporting out of the hospital to whatever fucking realm the reapers live in.

I wrap my arms around myself and wait, hating that I'm upset that he didn't say anything more, and even more upset that when he comes back, it will be the last time I see him.

When he pops back with Eros' pretentious plated quiver, he hands it to me and I take it clutching it against my chest.

"Thank you. And thank you for being my date to the ball." It feels like swallowing nails when I say it.

"Right. Is that it then?" he says, his tone angry.

I look up at his furious dark eyes and blink a few times. I teleport directly to the High Cupid's office, drop off the arrow, before going home and crying into the mountain of pillows and stuffed animals on my bed.

*S*he just wanted that stupid fucking quiver back. She acted like last night meant nothing, like I was nothing.

I'm slamming the cupboard in the break room and being a brooding asshole when Mors sits at the circular table. She slurps her coffee loudly and sighs an audible ah after each sip. I want to choke her.

"So I see that the cupids put you in an excellent mood."

I slam the door, pulling out the shitty instant coffee.

"I thought everything was going perfectly. But apparently I'm only good enough for one night. I'm good enough to use to piss off her stupid douche of an ex-boyfriend and parade around Cupidale like some dumbass on a leash. I was daft for thinking I could have anything more with a cupid." It all spews out of me embarrassingly fast, and I feel like Love for a moment. The way she talks super fast and spills her guts out, it makes my chest ache.

"I know for a fact the cupid didn't say all that depressing shit. What really happened?"

I run her through the entire night, leaving out some very graphic details until I get to the part when I was summoned to collect a soul.

"Wait. You're telling me you had the best sex of your life with this woman and you left her room without leaving a note?"

"I took… something else," I reply, not needing Mors to know all of what we did the other night.

"You think she realized you took something? She probably thinks you just wanted a one-night stand and nothing else because you fucking idiots didn't communicate. This is truly exhausting and why I never read the miscommunication trope."

"But she didn't say anything when she asked for Eros quiver," I argue.

"Yeah, because she probably had to put her poor little broken heart to the side to approach you in the first place. You didn't say anything either, you dumbass."

I blink at the reaper and piece everything together, how sad Love looked, how I didn't explain why I had to leave in the middle of the night and had no way to get back to her room.

"Shit," I hiss and Mors drinks more of her coffee loudly.

"You've lived too long to be this fucking stupid, Death."

"Thanks," I deadpan.

"As repayment, I'd like for her to set me up with one of her cupid friends once you have this all resolved."

I blink at her, trying to picture the grouchy reaper with someone as bubbly as a cupid.

She shrugs her shoulders and sips her coffee. "What can I say, I like pink." She winks, and I shake my head.

"I've got to find a way to talk to her." I say it more to myself than Mors.

"Seriously, do I have to spell everything out?" She rolls her eyes and I just stare at her, waiting for her to speak again. She finally breaks with a groan. "She never fulfilled your side of the bargain. Find the last person you want to make a love match with and summon her."

I grab the reaper's head and kiss the top of her dark hair. "Mors, you're a genius."

She shoves me off like I have a disease, and I laugh and teleport to Chinatown, knowing exactly who to use my last arrow on.

I pace back and forth, wondering what the probability of Mors being wrong is? What if Love truly just wanted a one-night thing and can't picture herself with a reaper for the long haul? She saw the disgust some of the cupids held for me at the party. It wouldn't be easy, but I know it would be worth it. Hopefully, she feels the same way and this is all some stupid misunderstanding.

Miss Guo is sitting in the back of the restaurant and it's only a matter of time before Mr. Xu comes with her delivery. Both of them lost their partners years ago and have been doing this little dance with one another. I know with Love's arrow they'll finally be able to get over whatever their hang up is. I also know Love will get serious joy out of making a true match.

I take a breath and summon Love as Mr. Xu walks through the back door. Miss Guo grins as they speak in rapid Mandarin.

Love teleports in front of me with a cloud of pink and an absolutely pissed off look on her face.

I grin. Mors was right. Thank fuck.

"What?" she asks, her hands on her hips.

"You still owe me an arrow," I tell her and point over at the pair speaking in the back of the store. Love softens for a moment and sighs, she automatically feels their connection, and even if she's pissed at me, there's no way she can deny I'm right about their pairing.

She doesn't respond to me, just pulls one arrow out, hitting Miss Guo first. She doesn't even bother with Mr. Xu—he didn't need a love arrow. The older couple touch hands and the older man leans down and kisses her. Love melts next to me for a moment, and then she stiffens.

"Is that all?" she says, looking down and not at me.

Communicate—properly—I remind myself.

I sigh and hold out the nipple clamp between my two fingers, the glittering color catching her attention.

"I didn't leave the other night because I wanted to. I was summoned to collect a soul and had no way of getting back to Cupidale. I took this, hoping you would realize and find me to get it back. I should have properly woken you up. I thought when you asked for Eros' stupid fucking quiver back it meant you wanted nothing to do with me." I word-vomit it all out and she takes the nipple clamp between her fingers and laughs.

"You thought I would notice you taking this?"

I shrug and my cheeks heat.

"I thought *you* wanted nothing to do with *me*," she says, looking down.

I cup her chin and force her to look up at me. I hate myself for ever making her doubt herself and that I even doubted what was between us.

"That couldn't be further from the truth. All night I thought about bringing up how much I enjoyed myself and couldn't imagine just having you for one night. I want you to be mine, Love."

Her eyes water, and she shakes her head.

"Did you steal that from the conversation heart pillow on my bed?"

I shrug and don't deny the claim.

"It won't be easy. Not everyone will accept a cupid and a reaper together," she states and I nod.

"It's worth it."

I mean it wholeheartedly. If any of the reapers dares to hurt her feelings, I'll make their life miserable. Love already seems to be able to handle herself effortlessly with the other cupids, and I couldn't care less about what they think.

"You really want me to be yours?"

"Yes, do you need me to prove it?"

She bites her full pink lip and nods; I grin and take her palm and teleport her back to my private rooms without a single word.

Where Love's room was bright, pink, and red, mine is the opposite. A large four-poster bed sits in the middle with black drapes and sheets to match. There aren't many personal effects, but it's comfortable and suits my needs.

Love clicks her tongue, and I feel like she might be slightly judging the impersonal nature of the room.

"I thought you were a reaper, not a vampire."

"I can bite, if you ask nicely," I whisper against the side of her face.

"You really didn't want to leave?" she asks in a soft, unsure voice.

"I'd never leave you. I want to take care of you, Love."

She swirls and faces me, and I swear to god there's little pink heart flecks in her eyes.

Love wraps her arms around herself, she almost looks a little insecure as she speaks. "That's all I ever wanted, someone who wants to take care of me, that isn't scared to take control. The other night was the best sex I've ever had."

"You want me to be your Daddy, little Love?" Might as well go all the way fucking in if we're doing this.

I swear a slight moan slips from her lips as she nods her head. "I think I'd like that very much."

"Thought you might," I say, while cupping her face. My thumbs glide along her cheekbones and her hands curl around my wrists. Love looks up at me with tear-filled eyes and I swipe a rogue tear away. "I don't want you crying anymore unless it's from taking my cock."

That makes her laugh, and she shakes away the sad emotion and smiles at me. A smiling, sweet Love is much better.

"I really thought you just wanted a one-night stand."

"Oh, little cupid, I want so much more than that. If you'll have me."

"I shouldn't have assumed."

"Me either. But I'm going to show you that you're mine. On your knees." The demand is dark, and I immediately know I'm the needy one in this relationship. I think I'm okay with that.

She shivers and falls to the floor like the obedient little cupid she is. Fuck, I'll never get tired of her pretty pink eyes looking up at me with desire and an eagerness to please. She's perfect, made for me. She's my reward for my long, service-filled life, I decide.

Her hands go to reach out for my robes, and while her earnestness is attractive, I quickly shut it down. A tendril of smoke wraps around her wrists. She gasps but places her now tied hands on her lap, her weight shifting from side to side.

"Do you like being tied up, baby?"

She shivers, of course she loves pet names, she's a fucking cupid.

"Yes, sir." She licks her lips and glances up at me.

I lean down and grip her chin, the loose fabric of my robes touching her chest, making her shiver.

"Not what I want to be called, baby."

"Yes, Daddy," she replies, shoving her hands in between her thighs and wiggling around.

"Who do you belong to?"

"You." It's a needy whisper and my cock twitches.

"That's right, just as I belong to you."

That makes her smile, and something inside of me cracks. I'm in love with the little cupid. I need her to leave my room understanding that we're a couple, that she's signing her soul over to be intertwined with mine.

"How many spankings should I give you for thinking I left with no intention of seeing you again?"

"I don't know. How many should I give you for not leaving a note or not saying anything when I came to get Eros—"

I grip her face roughly and stare at her for a long moment. It was innocent, I know it was, but she needs to learn early how things operate with me. I'm jealous and possessive, and the mention of that name triggers me.

"You don't say another's name when you're with me. Do you understand?" I keep my tone calm, not wanting to scare her. Love swallows and nods her head.

"Five for not believing in me, another five for the sass, and ten for saying his name."

Her mouth gapes open in disbelief, and I shut it with my thumb.

"That seems a little harsh."

I grin at her. "Harsh would be using the flogger. You're just getting my palm."

Her lips part again, and a little thrill fills me over this cupid and how absolutely perfect she is for me. I mean, I knew the cupids were incredibly open with their sexuality. However, I didn't know they would be into my same brand of pleasure. Between being with Love and what I saw at the party, that couldn't be further from the truth.

"You'd like that, wouldn't you, Love. My baby likes a little bit of pain with her pleasure?"

She nods, and I truly consider grabbing the flogger but don't; I'll save that for another night if she does something naughty.

I want to own Love. I want her to depend on me, for her to beg for me to punish her and then kiss it better. I want everything she's willing to give, and I plan on wringing her dry.

I easily pick her up and place her on her feet. My hand toys with her long soft hair, and I grab her gently on the back of her neck and lead her to the bed, where I sit first and pat my lap.

She looks down at her hands, and I tsk at her. "Those stay."

Love grumbles under her breath but stands between my legs, where I roll down her panties and push her pink sundress up to her hips. I kiss her mound before picking her up and tossing her over my lap. She squirms against my erection and uses her elbows for purchase against the bed as I attempt to expose her perfect ass.

"Vanish your wings," I tell her.

She has to breathe deeply a few times, but eventually she hides them. I forget she hasn't been a cupid for long. It probably takes her a lot of power to do that.

"Good girl," I tell her, finally getting an unobstructed view of her behind that is going to be a darker shade of pink once I'm done with her.

"Do you remember how many?" I ask.

"Like I could forget."

I swat her ass hard, and she gasps.

"That's for being a brat. Now the twenty start, and you're going to count for me, baby."

I can tell she wants to say something but thinks better of it. *Good girl.*

"If it's too much, tell me to stop and I will," I reassure her.

I drag my hand over the beautiful pink globe of her ass and squeeze. I can already see that her pussy is dripping for me, and I've barely touched her.

I raise my palm and smack her left cheek. It bounces and the sting of my hand has me biting back a groan.

"One," she whispers.

"Good."

I spank her again in the same spot, and she wiggles but still keeps counting. She doesn't beg or whine—she takes her punishment beautifully.

I'm an asshole as I hit the spot four more times and that's

when she breaks. Her voice turns into a rasp, and she attempts to shift on my lap. It only makes me harder.

She's panting, and I give her a moment of reprieve, pushing apart her ass cheeks and spitting on her tight, little back hole. My thumb slides along the spit as I toy with her, knowing I'm going to claim that hole soon enough.

"Who owns this ass?"

"You do," she says quickly.

I slide in a little more, hardly penetrating, and she pushes her ass towards my hand, pushing me deeper inside of her.

I pull my hand away, and she whines. It's like music to my ears as I slap her unblemished cheek four times in quick succession.

"Halfway there. You're being so good. I think I like your ass this shade of pink."

"Oh. God."

"Keep counting, little cupid."

I spank her upper thighs, the same spots I've been targeting, and lastly when we're on number twenty, I spank between her legs. She nearly shouts the word twenty while her body trembles on top of mine.

I soothe her sore ass, rubbing and kneading the tender flesh.

"Good girl, now you get a reward."

"Thank you, Daddy."

I think I die right then and there. But no reaper comes to collect my soul.

My ass is sore in all the best ways as Death tenderly rubs my flesh and praises me on a good job. I didn't think he could be more perfect than he was the other night, but I couldn't have been more wrong.

This reaper is everything I've ever wanted and more.

"Look at you, making a mess of my lap," he says in a tone that shows he's pleased, not degrading. "Are you feeling needy, baby?"

Gah, again with the baby. The daddy/baby combo is basically a perfect kill shot to my non-active ovaries.

"Please."

"Please, what?" he says.

"Please, Daddy." It flows off my tongue enthusiastically.

All I've ever wanted since becoming a cupid is for someone to care for me, while not underestimating me, and Death does that. He's proud of me, while also giving me the firm dominant hand that I've so desperately craved.

His hand slides over my ass and dips into my hot, needy pussy. He groans as his fingers toy with my clit and slide over my dripping entrance.

When his fingers slide into me, the only thing I can hear is the gush of my cunt wrapping around him and the thundering of my heartbeat.

"This pussy was made for me," he says, curling his fingers deep inside of me. "This too," he adds, sliding his thumb into my ass.

He's relentless with his hands as he fucks in and out of me, his fingers hitting that perfect spot until I'm writhing and nearly crying on top of him. I try to release my hands, but whatever shadow magic he possesses is too strong. I'm at his mercy as I ride out my orgasm against his hand.

Trembles rip through me as he slows his speed, but doesn't slide out of me. He wants to feel every single flutter of my release against his fingers and that just makes me feel even more endeared to him.

"That's it," he coos.

The wetness that drips down my thighs and with the drag of his fingers is obscene. He easily lifts me so that I'm straddling his lap. He's still fully clothed, and my dress is pushed to my hips.

His large, strong hands grip the back of my neck as he crashes his lips against mine. The kiss is searing; it feels like a delicious claim, and I can't get enough of it. I want his lips pressed against mine as much as I possibly can.

With my hands tied, I can still fist his robes, but nothing else.

He snaps his fingers, and the bondage disappears along with his clothes and mine.

"How?" I ask, blinking at him.

"I've been around for a very long time, Love."

"Ah, a good ole age gap romance," I joke, and he smiles.

I can't help but cup his cheek with my hand. There's a darkness that follows him around, but I feel like I bring some much needed lightness to his life. I want to make his life better in any way I can. I can't imagine that his job is easy, and if my obedience and tenderness can bring him some joy I'll do whatever I can.

"You're my girl, so yes, I'll concede to an age gap romance," he says, and I bite my lip.

"Opposites attract, size difference, age gap, and don't forget insta-lust."

"It was not insta-lust."

"When we met you were staring at my tits the same way you are right now," I say, poking his chest.

He just grins and pushes my breasts together and looks down at them.

"Can you blame me?"

"No, they are pretty perfect."

"Ride my cock and let me come on them," he says quickly, and I laugh.

"And they say romance is dead."

"Never. Not when there are pretty cupids with huge tits flying around," he says.

I laugh, but he cuts it off when he leans forward and kisses and sucks each nipple tenderly. Needing him, I slide a hand between us and fist his cock before slowly sliding down his length.

He breathes against my chest, making the saliva he left behind cold, and I shiver.

His hands slide from my breasts to my ass, and I wince as he squeezes. The smug bastard just smiles, knowing I'm tender from where he spanked me.

"You're so fucking perfect, baby," he says while looking at me with lust-filled eyes.

"You feel so good," I praise him. His lips part, and his hands grip tighter against my flesh.

My hands are holding on tight to the back of his neck as I ride him. My clit grinds back and forth against his neatly trimmed curls, and I know I'm close.

"Make a mess on Daddy's cock," he grits out.

It breaks me and I shatter on top of him, my body trembling as I tug on his hair and press kisses against the side of his face.

"That's it. Give it to me," he groans, tugging on my ass and hair.

My orgasm feels like it lasts forever. Maybe it's the sensitivity from earlier or how much more real this all feels, knowing there are emotions attached. I'm going to be the most spoiled cupid there ever was if it always feels like this, which I know it will.

Death clutches me against his chest as I shake on top of him. I hold him just as close, wanting every inch of our bodies to touch. He kisses the side of my face and his hands are gentle as he strokes my hair and back, knowing I need a second.

His dick twitches inside of me, and I groan into his neck.

"You drive me fucking crazy," he says.

"Feeling's mutual, reaper."

Before I know it, he's sliding out of me and pushing me on my back. He grins down and climbs on top, his legs balanced on each side of me.

"Push those pretty tits together, cupid," he demands.

I nod and do as I'm told; he takes a minute to just stare down at my naked body, and I do the same. He's a work of art, and with him on top of me like this, I feel so soft and small.

His cock is covered in a sheen of moisture from fucking me, and he uses that to push in between my breasts.

He moans, watching himself disappear in and out of my breasts pushed together and I know he won't last long. I like having this power over him, knowing that we're both endlessly attracted to one another and that it's more than just physical.

I'm feeling like a menace as I speak, knowing it will send him over the edge.

"Thank you, Daddy."

He falls apart on top of me, panting as he pulls out and strokes his cock so that rivulets of cum cover my chest. It's warm and sticky in the best way as he wrings out every drop before looking down at the mess he's made of me.

"Fuck, I wish I had one of those human phones. I understand the appeal now," he says, just staring at my cum-covered chest. Sadly, no camera can take pictures of beings in the veil, and I suddenly wish they could as well.

His two fingers slide through his release as he rubs himself into my chest. As soon as he's convinced he's marked me enough, he slides the two fingers in my mouth, which I greedily suck down.

"You're fucking perfect, Love."

He collapses to the side of me, tugging my back against his chest and nuzzling his face into the crook of my neck.

"Bath?" he asks, and I nod, his cum drying on my tits is becoming slightly uncomfortable.

He hops off the bed and picks me up like I weigh nothing as he carries me to the bathroom. It's no surprise that the space is dark: black and gray marble fills the space, and he sits me on the lip of the tub as he runs the water.

"I don't have anything to put in it," he says with disapproval. "I'll get some of that girly shit next time I'm out."

I bite my lip and nod, liking that he wants to go out of his way to do things for me. I'll never turn down being spoiled, especially if he wants to be called Daddy, then he needs to live up to the name.

The water fills, and he climbs in first, holding a hand out to me, and I follow. My back is pressed against his chest as the warm water washes against my achy body.

Death kisses my shoulder softly as we just relax in silence.

"We live in different realms," I say suddenly.

"We'll make it work, take turns staying at one another's places. I'll reach out and see if there's any way to portal directly to each other's realms. If not, we can just have a mutual meeting place every night."

I smile at his thoughtfulness, but I'm truly not tied to Cupidale if I'm being honest. Besides Amore, there isn't much waiting for me, and we're partnered up often for assignments. I'll see her all the time.

"Or I could stay here. I don't get summoned like you do. I just have quotas. But your room needs a lot of work," I say.

Death stiffens behind me for a moment before his arms tighten.

"You'd really live here with me?"

"Assuming I can redecorate, then yes."

"Baby, you can do whatever you want," he whispers, and I sink deeper into the water.

We stay in the tub for a ridiculously long time before we decide we need to eat and I need to figure out how I'm going to get all my belongings to his apartment.

My hair is still wet, and I know I look like I got royally fucked as Death holds my hand and leads me to a small little break room that's down the hallway from his apartment.

I'm shocked to find two other reapers sitting there: one is a man, and the other is an attractive, yet slightly terrifying woman.

"That's Mors and Demise," Death says. "This is Love." The way he says my name is so sweet and precious, I'm about ready to drag him back to his room and fuck his brains out all over again.

"You know, I genuinely thought you were making that shit up," Demise, the male reaper says.

Mors gives me a polite enough smile as she sips her coffee. I swear she gives Death a conspiratorial look.

I swear to god, if she's been with Death before, I'll poke her beautiful brown eyes out. I must be glaring at the reaper because she laughs, throwing her head back.

"He's not my type. But you," she says looking me up and down, "Death, you might have competition."

I grin at that and sit at the table next to the very forward reaper. Even if I'm with Death, and there's no changing that I'm still a vain cupid, it's nice to be admired.

"I'm currently off the market."

"She'll be staying off the market," Death grumbles, placing a mug of what looks like sludge in front of me.

"But I do have some pretty friends," I tell Mors, and she smiles.

"There are other cupids willing to date outside of Cupidale?" she teases.

"I think so, yes."

"Then count me in."

Death doesn't look surprised by the conversation at all, he just rolls his eyes and throws a hand on the back of my chair. His fingers toy with my hair, and man does it feel nice to be receiving so much delicious physical touch.

"What are you two love birds going to do now?" Mors asks.

"I'm taking Love on a date," Death says casually, like we already discussed this. When in fact we have not and I'm lowkey freaking out about it.

I mean, sure, we basically agreed that I'm moving in, and there was some daddy kink and spanking… but a date… a date is the real deal. That's romance, that's how people who are together forever keep the flame alive.

"Oh, don't look so shocked," Death says, rubbing his thumb along my shoulder.

"Where are we going?"

"I figured we could go to the aquarium, use some love arrows and then maybe hang out around the Red Lobster later."

I gape at him, so do his two reaper companions.

Mors whistles. "Red Lobster, that's a serious commitment right there."

I can't tell if she's being serious or not, but all the humans who want to go to the next level always go to Red Lobster, it's way better than Red Robin. The gesture is romantic and perfect and I fall even more in love with the reaper.

"I'd love nothing more," I tell Death.

"Me too," he replies and I get the double meaning.

Here in a different realm surrounded by a bunch of reapers, I realize that love isn't dead and Valentine's Day goes back to securing its place as my favorite holiday.

One Year Later

J'm sitting on Death's lap, my tight red dress a stark contrast against his black tuxedo. He looks fucking delicious, and as soon as that heart drops, I'm going to fall on my knees and—

"Patience, baby," he whispers in my ear.

I shift on his lap. How dare he ask me to be patient when we both know I'm currently sitting here with a heart-shaped butt plug and nearly dripping, waiting for him to ravish me?

"Have you seen yourself?"

The man is usually naked or in his robes in my presence, but in this getup? My mind has nearly melted. He looks like James Bond or Batman. No, definitely Batman.

"Yes, I have, you're one lucky cupid," he says with a grin.

"Oh, my fuck. Please stop paying this arrogant bastard compliments. Isn't his head big enough?" Mors complains, jostling a very happy Juliet on her lap.

She's up for the rookie lover of the year. I couldn't be prouder of the cupid she's become. I almost feel bad for Eros in his own way. He's a bit of a good luck Chuck. Once you've been with him, you basically toss away cupid kind and find the reaper of your dreams. I'm certainly not complaining.

I'm not up for any awards this year, and I totally get why. I've been engrossed in my whirlwind inter-veil-being relationship.

While I think it's made me a better cupid all around, I haven't been as focused on the numbers game, more so getting it right with my arrows. Making love matches has become far more fulfilling than spreading lust, even if I still start an orgy from time to time.

It also doesn't hurt that my guy secretly enjoys helping me find true love matches. It's honestly the perfect setup because a lot of the time we work to help people find love after the hardest time of their life.

I nestle against my big softy of a reaper, and both of his hands wrap around my hips as he kisses my head.

"Your head isn't super big, just slightly large," I sigh, and he swats my ass.

"Little cupid, I will spank your ass for each number of the countdown if you can't behave."

Breaking the rules absolutely has its benefits, but Death has his rules. He totally would spank me in front of these cupids to make a point, but he won't fuck me. He has no issue showing his dick, or me drooling all over it either. I found that out very quickly during the May Day Parade.

But the reaper doesn't like others watching while he's inside of me. He says it's just for us. My romance is absolutely sickening in the best way. I know, I adore it.

Cupiō takes his stand in front of the cupids. Same speech, same awards, until we get to the Rookie of the Year.

Mors holds on tight to her cupid, and when Juliet's name is announced, they embrace, both of them with massive smiles on their faces.

"Go get your award, honey," the usually grumpy reaper says to Juliet. Juliet kisses Mors one more time while Death and I clap and she goes up to get her award.

Mors looks on with hearts in her eyes, and I can't help but sigh at the precious love surrounding us.

"Stop looking at me like that, Love," Mors complains.

"I can't help it. You two are just so fucking precious. It feels like my cupid heart might burst all over the floor from watching you together."

Death chuckles, and Mors glares at me. She still has a long way to go with being around cupids. But the effort she put into her appearance with her slick black suit just shows me she cares tremendously for Juliet. I'm so smart for setting them up together.

"Are you boasting inside of your own head?" Death says, squeezing my ass and making me shift back to being aware of the toy inside of me.

"Can you blame me?"

"No, baby, I can't. You're amazing," he whispers against my ear, and kisses that sweet soft spot right below my earlobe.

Falling absolutely wings over feet for Death has been the easiest thing I've done as a cupid, and I'm better for it. It's not the type of romance where you get so lost that you can't find yourself. It's the type where you grow alongside each other. We're both better people because we're together. I never truly understood how much support meant in a long-lasting relationship, but it's everything.

Love isn't about the gifts… though I do really like gifts. The dates, which I also need at least every week. But the true grit to making a relationship last is loving the other person for who they are and always having their back. We're each other's biggest cheerleaders, and I wouldn't trade it for anything in the world.

Juliet comes back to the table, her bright shiny gold award glistening as she sits back on Mors lap. Their foreheads are pressed together as they speak sweetly to one another, and I turn over to look at Death.

His beautiful face continues to take my breath away.

"Did you have a good Love New Year, Love?" he asks, his nose dragging along the side of my face.

"The best I could have asked for," I whisper back, and his lips meet mine.

He kisses me softly, tenderly, though I know his plans tonight are not sweet. Don't get me wrong, sometimes we make precious slow love together, but for big nights, like tonight, we always like to play.

Especially since Death went to the High Reaper and asked for tomorrow off. I have a feeling he's going to dehydrate me with all the nasty, messy things he wants to do with me.

"Whatever you're thinking, yes, I'll give it to you," he says against my lips and I smile.

Lavender Haze by Taylor Swift comes on and I pop up off his lap and grab his hand. He tries to hide a smile as he follows me to the dance floor and I sway. He's behind me, grabbing my hips and hunching over me, moving with the music. It always makes my heart flutter the way he'll dance with me, even though I know it's not his favorite thing.

Amore is grabbing my hand as she dances in front of Doe. I love that Doe is shorter than her. It's fucking cute.

We're all smiling like idiots, and I nearly burst into tears with how happy I am at this moment. This is all I ever wanted. I finally truly feel like a cupid.

Nearly every cupid in the place is singing the song at the top of their lungs as we dance. I laugh when I look at Mors, who seems absolutely dumbfounded by everything going on, but she dances with her cupid nonetheless.

The song switches to *My Love Mine All Mine* by Mitski, and I twirl in Death's arms so he can hold me while we slow dance.

I feel safe and cherished in his arms, and like always, when we're together, we're in a soft pink bubble of bliss.

Death cradles the back of my head with a strong hand, guiding me to look up at his handsome face.

"Thank you for letting me love you, Love."

"Fuck, I can't cry at the Valentine's Day Ball," I complain, and his fingers rub my jaw.

"It doesn't count if they're happy tears."

"You're right." I sniffle, burying my face in his large, impressive chest. I place my chin there and look back up at him. "Loving you is the easiest thing I've ever done. And you're welcome."

He grins, cupping my face and rubbing my jaw as we sway with the music. He smiles so much now—only for me—and it lights my soul on fire every time. I'm not sure if an eternity in the veil is enough time with him.

There are a few more songs and Death obliges me by dancing, or at least touching me and swaying as the music plays.

The countdown begins, the surrounding noise is loud, but all I can do is look up at the love of my life.

The heart drops, confetti and balloons everywhere as we ring in the new year with a searing kiss.

He picks me up by my middle to bring our lips together, and I wrap my arms around his broad shoulders. Death squeezes one of my ass cheeks, and I yelp while the man smiles against my lips.

"What am I going to do with you tonight, Love?"

"Whatever you want, Daddy," I reply with a smirk.

He kisses me again passionately as debauchery begins to unfold around us.

"I love you," he whispers in my ear and I shiver.

"I love you too."

"Happy Love New Year."

"It's going to be the best one yet," I say as I crash my lips to his.

He swings me around and portals us to our room. It's no longer the dreary black disaster it was previously, now it's perfect. I let him keep the black sheets, but the bed is covered in pink and red pillows and stuffed animals. There's a pink bean bag chair next to a leather recliner and our bookshelf. Now I just have to convince him to let us get a hellcat. I'm working endlessly on convincing him it's what the space needs.

"Didn't feel like showing anyone what's mine tonight," he murmurs as he pushes me against the bed. My fists clench in the soft sheets as he pushes my dress up my hips. He stares at my panties for a quick moment before smacking my ass and laughing. "Cheeky, cupid," he says with another smack.

"They're cute, don't you think?"

"The cutest," he says as he rolls off the panties I made that say Daddy Death on them. His teeth graze my ass cheek as he grabs the heart-shaped base of the plug. He doesn't take it out, just slowly pressing in and out. I can't start begging this early, so I just let him play with me as I wait patiently.

He leaves me on the bed, and I know better than to get up before he tells me to, so I just lie there until I hear the telltale hum of a vibrating wand.

Fuck, I'm in for it tonight.

He lifts my hips and places the wand between me and the mattress. I automatically gasp as it hits my clit, and he chuckles lowly at the torture he's imposing on me.

The wand is buzzing and his hands are feverishly touching me all over before he goes back to being fascinated with the butt plug.

"Make a mess and I'll fuck you while keeping this in," he whispers, accentuating his words by pushing the toy harder into me and upping the setting of the wand.

I'm moaning and writhing on the bed and the man just holds me down, just watching my pussy drip and my ass clench.

"Good girl, come for Daddy."

He always knows how to break me. I fall apart. The orgasm lasts longer with the plug and my pussy aches to be filled up as it pulsates around nothing.

Death removes the wand and pushes into me completely clothed. I have to nearly break my neck to get a good look at him in his tux while he enters me, and phew, I'm ready to come all over again.

"God, your cunt is so tight," he groans, and I mumble some nonsense.

With the stretch of his impressive cock and the toy in my ass, I feel like I might simply shatter.

It's clear this first round isn't going to last long as his strong pelvis slaps against my ass.

He makes these delicious masculine moans and I'm so close. Death curls his body over mine, pushing my dress out of the way to play with my clit as he fucks me.

"Happy Valentine's Day, baby," he says against my ear as he thrusts.

I come on the spot and he tumbles after, filling me with his come. We stay like that for a moment, panting and drained as he rubs my skin, making sure I'm okay.

When he pulls out, we both wince. He's gentle as he pulls the plug out and disappears our clothes so we can lie in our bed together.

His head rests on Sager the Puppy, the Squishmallow he got me this Valentine's Day, and I grin ear to ear.

"Whoever would have thought I'd domesticate a reaper?"

He leans down to bite my neck and I laugh endlessly as he presses his body on top of mine, love in his eyes as he kisses me.

"I'd do anything for you, little cupid. Be mine?"

I grin, loving our inside joke as I bite my lip and nod my head. "Forever and always."

He makes love to me all day long, and I can't help but think that sometimes petty pays off tenfold.

ALSO BY SARAH BLUE

Other works by Sarah Blue

Dead Palms MC Omegaverse

Nobody's Darlin'

Pucked Up Omegaverse

One Pucked Up Pack

Don't Puck With My Heart

Puck Around & Find Out - Date TBD

Heat Haven Omegaverse

Heat Haven

Omega's Obsession

Protector's Promise

Too Tempting

Heat Haven Holidays

Want to take a walk on the paranormal side?

Charming Your Dad

Charming the Devil

Charming as Hell

The Carlson Brothers - Contemporary Romance

Swallow Your Pride

Forget Your Morals - Coming 2024

ACKNOWLEDGMENTS

Leisha - For always reading early and dealing with my chaotic writing schedule.

Fallon & Kassie - For being such amazing, supportive, bad ass bitches.

Stephanie, Kim, Lindsay - Thank you for helping me work out some kinks (no pun intended)

Sandra - For my beautiful cover and for basically forcing me to write this.

Ava, Megan, Stacha, Hailey - For jumping in and making sure the ebook looks great before surprise dropping this.

And lastly... to the heart shaped nipple clamps that have been living rent free since I found them online when researching for this story.

ABOUT THE AUTHOR

Sarah Blue writes contemporary sweet omegaverse, erotic, why choose romances. She loves romance in nearly any genre. When she isn't writing you can find her nose buried in a book or lit up from her kindle. She loves the sweeter side of romance and creating interesting characters while adding adventure and spice. Writing strong female characters and male characters willing to show weakness is something that makes her gooey on the inside.

Sarah lives in Maryland with her husband, two sons, and two annoying cats. If she isn't reading or writing she is probably working on a craft project or scrolling on Tik Tok.

Tik Tok/Instagram - @sarahblueauthor
Website - authorsarahblue.com
Facebook Group - Sarah Blue's Reader Group